DeSai

Lucien's Reign

By
R.W.K. Clark

This is a work of fiction. All names, characters, locales, and incidents are
the product of the author's imagination and any resemblance to actual
people, places or events is coincidental or fictionalized.
Published in the United States by Clarkltd.
Po Box 45313 Rio Rancho, NM 87174
info@clarkltd.com

Edition 1

United States Copyright Office
TX8-281-477 May 2016
Library of Congress Control Number: 2017907154
International Standard Book Numbers
ISBN-10: 069272219X
ISBN-13: 978-0692722190
ASIN: B01GD7CWLI

/200801

CONTENTS

ACKNOWLEDGMENTS

I dedicate this novel to my wonderful readers and for all the amazing people I've met and those I haven't. To my family and loved ones, all your support will not be forgotten.

This book was made possible by reviews from readers like you.

Thank you

R.W.K. Clark

PROLOGUE

Cyril DeSai was a winemaker from the French region in the 16th century. He had a wife and two children, and he was one of the most esteemed businessmen in all of France.

One day, when Cyril went out to the fields, he discovered the vineyards guard dogs had been torn apart, rows of his grapes had been violently destroyed, and his family was brutally murdered. In his efforts, he was bitten, in the night during his search, by a vampire.

For the next several centuries, Cyril DeSai roamed the Earth. He tried to build a family, and he sought one to be his Queen. In eternal pain he would start a family, only to be discovered as a direct result of the sloppiness of his own 'children.' He would be hunted, chased, and forced to take shelter in his cave in the side of a cliff on the oceans of Honduras. He ached each and every time from the loss of what he had begun, but Cyril knew that his survival was most important if he was ever to bring to fruition what his own instincts drove him to do.

Build a family.

Cyril came into his own finally, and the world became his, but now he discovered that his family, his children, needed a mother and that as King he needed a Queen. He began to be driven to find her, and it was with a relentless passion he went through women, seeking, searching, and hoping to find love with that one woman, who was nameless and faceless to him for so long.

But yes, he did find her. Rasia Engres came to him when he least expected it when he was fully coming into all that was destined to be his, even if it was all a temporary gift. He found the perfect woman to mother his family and cement his kingdom. She was much more than he understood; she was more than a woman, unbeknownst to the King of the Vampires.

She was a witch, raised by the Powers, and destined to rule the world. She knew of her destiny: find a vampire, if they do exist, and take their gift of life immortal.

She devoted herself to learning all she could about this unknown, and undiscovered breed. She studied and sought. She obsessed and lost sleep, and in between, she killed to satisfy the evil inside of her. Yes, she was a witch, but she was perfect for the job which she had been chosen for. She would do so much more than finding a vampire and take his life for her kind.

DeSai made a grave mistake, and he knew it.

His love, his queen, was not his at all. He looked into her eyes sadly, and for the first time since he discovered the bodies of his wife and children hundreds of years ago, a single tear fell from his eye.

As he had looked at her, that tear falling, his dead

heart began to pound harder, and in a split second, she reached out and ripped his head from his body.

She had fully come into her power. Now it was her responsibility to see to it that the facts about her lover live on. She would not let him die on the floor of that basement office at Cliffside Wineries; she would keep his memory, and his love for her, alive.

R.W.K. Clark

CHAPTER 1

Beads of sweat gathered on her forehead and trickled down her face, soaking into the pillow beneath her head. She writhed in pain for what seemed like minutes at a time, then she would relax, moaning and breathing heavily. Rasia had never experienced such intense pain in her life; she thought she would surely die as a result of this child escaping her body.

Another wave of pain began to torment her slowly, creeping up on her body and perpetuating into unbearable agony. She squirmed violently like trying to get away from it as if trying to escape it. Her back arched off of the mattress, and a desperate scream escaped her lips.

Two women, members of the family, were by her side. One, Agatha Cross, sat on the bed next to her, wiping her forehead with a cool cloth and stroking her arm with love. She made noises that were meant to be comforting, but in her tortured state, all of this behavior only served to aggravate and infuriate her. Rasia jerked her arm, throwing Agatha's hand from it as she growled, "Shut up!"

The other woman, Deborah Castle, stood at the foot

of the bed in silence. She had been a nurse before her position became extinct in the world; now she served only to birth the children born of family members. It was a full-time job in itself, and she used to love it. Now, standing at the feet of the Queen herself, she thought she may implore Rasia DeSai to allow her to pursue other avenues.

The wave of pain had passed, and Rasia had almost dozed off in her exhaustion before another swept her up. She began to feel the overwhelming desire to push this monster from her body, and she began to grunt and bear down in cooperation with the urge.

Finally, the forsaken child would arrive. Rasia had thought that perhaps the passage of time during her pregnancy would provide her with some feeling for the child that resembled love, but it never happened. She had spent the last nine months dreading this birth, and now she found herself dreading the child's life.

"She is ready," Deborah told Agatha quietly. She took a towel from a stack on a small folding table which had been placed next to her post, then she got down on her knees at the foot of the bed and placed her hands flat on the soles of Rasia's perfect feet.

"Bear down… push!" she told her Queen.

Rasia's face crumpled in pain, and she began to push with all of her might, using Deborah's hands, and great stature, for leverage. She pushed as much as she could, but then collapsed back onto her pillow, crying and gasping for breath. The urge came again, taking over her thoughts and controlling her entire being.

Deborah spoke again. "Again, my Queen."

Rasia's head and shoulders left her pillow as her feet began to push violently against Deborah's hands once again. Her pained groan as she pushed was filled with an unworldly growl; how she wanted this beast out of her body. He had done nothing but grieve her since his conception.

The baby's head crowned, and a pleased smile crossed Deborah's face. "His head. I see it now!"

Agatha held Rasia's hand in both of hers, and as Rasia clenched it painfully, the woman smiled a toothy grin. Their new king would soon arrive. Their new Master was almost here!

When Rasia heard that his head was visible, she got a second wind. She held Agatha's hand in her crushing grip, grabbing a handful of bedding in her other hand. Her head and shoulders once again left the bed, and she looked Deborah in the eyes, her own emerald eyes on fire with both pain and determination.

"I have had enough of this," she growled. "Let's get this over with."

With that, Rasia bore down with all of her strength. The boy's head came immediately, and Deborah attempted to clear his throat, thinking that Rasia would breathe, but she did not. Instead, her pushing gained even more momentum, and in seconds, the child's shoulders were out, and he shot from Rasia's body like a bullet from a gun.

She looked at the clock on her nightstand on the right, its numerals glowing red: it was exactly twelve midnight.

Now Rasia collapsed, laughing almost hysterically with relief. Agatha busied herself with wiping sweat from her Queen's head and shoulders while Deborah set about finishing the job before her. The placenta would be kept, for the Queen would offer it to the Powers. After she had obtained it, she placed it according to Rasia's instructions, then wrapped the child, bloody and covered with water and mucus, in a flannel. She stood and gazed at him as he screamed. His hair was as black as night; he was quite beautiful.

She walked around to the side of the bed and held the swaddled boy out to his mother. "Your son, my Queen," she began.

"Take him!" Rasia spat. "I will get to him when I am ready." Her eyes remained closed and her face calm, but her voice reeked of hatred.

Deborah's eyes grew wide, but she kept her voice steady. "He will need to eat…"

Now Rasia's eyes opened, and she looked at the nurse angrily. "Then do what has to be done. Put him at my breast if you must, but let me be," she told her. "And don't leave my side. When he is finished, take him away."

Deborah obeyed, placing the boy at his mother's breast to feed, laying him on a pillow for support. He rooted around for her nipple, his eyes closed, his perfect little arms and legs flailing in the linen. He found it and latched on quickly, sucking for what appeared to be dear life. Once he settled, Deborah began to clean him off with a warm, wet facecloth while Agatha plumped pillows and made the new mother more comfortable.

Rasia settled in and finally opened her eyes as Agatha began to gently brush her long red tresses. She smiled slightly at the woman in thanks, an unusual gesture for their Queen. Then she turned her attention to Deborah. "You have done well."

After what seemed like an eternity, she looked down at her son. A look of disgust crossed her face; it was enough to surprise her servants, but they kept it to themselves. Rasia continued to stare at him; so this was the creature that would take her throne. She hated him instantly. He looked like his father, whom Rasia missed desperately, but he was born to take away the power she had gained through his father's death, and that made her sick to her stomach. All she had plotted and schemed for, and finally come into, would eventually be handed to this… child. She glanced down at his face for a moment; his eyes were not the eyes of a newborn. He looked at her as if he knew her and all that was inside of her.

But she must protect him, she knew. She must teach him and nurture him, for this was the will of the Powers. She had no choice in the matter, and to defy their will would mean only certain death for her. He was chosen for this; it was his sole purpose. She had served most of hers, and now she would spend her life completing it by seeing him to the throne.

He was a monster.

After a short time, the boy began to squirm; he was

finished. Deborah immediately took him into the bathroom to clean him up better and get him out of his mother's sight. She showed no true affection for the child, and Deborah wanted him to be away from her, just as her Queen wished. Rasia turned to Agatha, her smile gone.

"You can go now," she said quietly. "You will be rewarded and recognized for your services." With that, Agatha left the room, as silent as a ghost.

Rasia relaxed and stared at the ceiling, resigning herself to her future. She would eventually become a slave to this child; that was what it boiled down to. She thought of her late husband Cyril; he would have been ecstatic at this moment. Alone, she was destined to hate what awaited her because every intention of her heart had been evil and selfish.

How she wished he were with her now. When she thought back to the night they spent together in Cyril's office, the night this boy was conceived, she experienced grief so deep that she thought she may die from it. How could she have taken the life of the only man, the only person, she had ever related to in her life? Even as she thought about the newborn, her stomach became sick with her thoughts.

The bathroom door opened and Deborah appeared with a clean bundle in her arms, swaddled in black. "I will take him out, Queen, but I will need to know what name you have given him. The family will want to know, for they will celebrate his arrival this very night."

Rasia looked the nurse over. "Let me see the boy

again."

Deborah brought him to his mother. Rasia did not make any attempt to take him from the woman; there would be plenty of time for that later. The nurse moved his swaddling away from his face and leaned down. Rasia looked at him closely.

Even in his brand new state, he was the spitting image of his father. His hair was as black as a raven's feathers, and his tiny nose was a reflection of Cyril's directly. Suddenly, the newborn opened his eyes and looked directly at her. There was no question in her mind. It did not matter that he was less than thirty minutes old; the child seemed to know what was going on.

His eyes were bright green, just as Rasia's were, and for a fraction of a second, she felt a wave of love. "Take him to the nursery and fetch his nanny. Let her know I will be with them when I have cleaned up and rested a bit."

The nurse straightened herself out and covered the boy's face once again, preparing to leave the room. She was just preparing to close the door behind her when Rasia spoke.

"Deborah," she began.

The nurse stopped in her tracks. "Yes, Queen?"

"His name is Lucien. Lucien Cerebus DeSai," she told her. "Now go."

Deborah bowed her head and closed the door behind her, leaving Rasia DeSai to come to terms with her destiny.

R.W.K. Clark

CHAPTER 2

The wheels of the buggy rolled smoothly over the concrete walkway in the private courtyard of the White House. The sun was shining brightly, its rays reflecting off the blue waters in the pond nearby, and they dazzled off the drops of dew which covered the grass.

It was indeed a beautiful morning. Rasia loved her early walks with little Lucien; in reality, she considered them the best part of their relationship. He was always his most quiet during these times, taking in all that was around him. For a child of twenty months, he was very intelligent and alert. Sometimes it seemed as though he was wise beyond his years, and it frightened her.

She had taken her fear to the Powers many, many times. Deep inside she longed for them to allow her to give the boy to one of her minions to raise, but the Powers had been adamant in their denial. She would raise the boy; it was her job alone, and no other would be permitted to do it.

They arrived at a gazebo at the end of the courtyard; this was her preferred place to be. She put the brakes on the buggy and freed Lucien from his restraints so he could run and play. As she fumbled with the clasps, he gazed at her, looking directly into her eyes. She returned his look uncomfortably; she always felt as though he were watching her and assessing her actions. Yes, this made her squirm emotionally, but it was the least of her concerns.

As of late, she had begun to… smell his blood, and it caused her great torment. When she caught its scent, it was as if she were a starving derelict who was visiting a buffet, but she was not allowed to eat. It was sheer torture, and she had to get far from him when this happened. To harm the boy would mean death. Other times she looked at him and what would come over her could be compared only to a mother's love. She would feel so much affection, and a sense of obligation, that she felt she would be overwhelmed by the emotions.

This is what she felt at this moment as she stood him on his feet on the ground. "Go, child! Enjoy the day!" She smiled at him, and he smirked at her in return before turning and running off like a shot, giggling like crazy. She found her smile grew at his child-like behavior. She may as well try to enjoy the little things.

Rasia took her place inside the gazebo and closed her eyes, breathing in the fresh morning air. It was cool and crisp, and it seemed to clear the fog from her mind, enabling her to think more clearly. It was priceless to her.

Lucien had been an easy child so far. While he would be too soon, he always seemed much older than he was. He was always deep in thought, and even though he could already speak in clear sentences, he rarely spoke to her. She knew this made her feel unloved and unwanted by him, but in all reality, she neither truly loved nor wanted him either. She was simply going through the motions.

"Mama…" Rasia's eyes snapped open, and she turned to the sound of her son's voice.

"Yes, Lucien?"

He held her eyes. "I heard noises in your room last night."

Rasia's heart began to pound, but she kept herself calm. "You were having a dream, Lucien. Remember when we talked about dreams?" Rasia stated.

He kicked his toe against the side of the gazebo while he looked at her; he was thinking on what she said. Suddenly, the tiny boy smirked slightly and shook his head, holding her gaze all the while.

"No, I was awake," he said, his wicked grin spreading before he then ran off to play once again.

Rasia took a deep breath as she realized she was shaking. He heard noises, indeed! She looked out over the horizon. What if he had? The look on his face told her he knew she was lying. Yes, he had heard noises.

About two months after Lucien's birth, Rasia began to feel the strong pull of sexual lust once again. It had lessened as her pregnancy had come closer to term, and it disappeared altogether for a time. But when the boy was two months old, it returned full force, and it was constantly unbearable. She could not satisfy it with any lover, and she had taken many since its return, both men and women.

Now she turned her attention back to the boy. How it angered her that his attitude with her was so intimidating, condescending, and aloof! She did not know how to deal with it. Well, now she knew she would have to be much more careful when it came to her activities after he retired. She would speak to her assistant about her options, as her activities were necessary to her well-being. She would not compromise on this, not for anyone, especially the twenty-month-old Lucien.

The boy played eagerly on yard toys for the next half-hour. This was really the only time of day when he appeared to be a real child, so she relished it immensely. These moments, stolen from time itself, were really the only things that kept her from completely ravaging the tot just to taste his blood.

Cyril would be appalled, and the thought made her laugh out loud. The very things Cyril had adored about her would surely disgust him today if he were here to share these times with her, but he was not. Who knew? Maybe if Cyril were here with her and Lucien, she would not experience these temptations and cravings at all. She knew that even though she had been the one to steal her husband's life, she was the one blaming him for her troubles now.

Lucien turned to her as she laughed, observing her happiness. "Is it time, Mama?"

Rasia got her wits about her. "Yes, Lucien. We will go in now."

He ran back to her and allowed her to put him back

into his buggy. He watched her as she buckled him in, as he always did. He felt a stirring in his stomach. When he looked at her, he felt angry, almost to the point of causing her physical pain somehow. He knew the things she thought, how she wanted his blood. He had no idea why, but the knowledge made him hate her all the more.

As they made their way to the house, Lucien said, "Mama, I want to play with the kitty when we get there."

Rasia's eyebrows lifted. He had never asked to play with Jax before. Jax was Rasia's cat, and though she had tried to share him with Lucien, the boy had never shown interest. His request pleased her. "Yes, Lucien, I would love to share Jax with you."

Once they were inside Rasia took the boy and placed him in the room which served solely as Jax's quarters. Once she had settled them together, she left the room and closed the door. Lucien's nanny, Desirae, stood quietly at her side. "They may play together," Rasia told the girl. "I will go have my bath, and I will return when I am finished."

With that, Rasia made her way to her room for her bath, a smile on her face. Lucien wanted to play with her cat! Perhaps he was warming up to her and her interests after all. She felt a glimmer of hope as she got into the hot water, and she soaked comfortably, a smile on her face.

∞

"Queen, Queen!" Desirae's voice cut through Rasia's daydreaming. She jumped, water splashing slightly, and grabbed her towel from the stand next to the bathtub. The bathroom door burst open, and Desirae stood before her, fear and panic all over her face.

Rasia was angry at the imposition and lashed out at the young nanny. "How do you presume to interrupt me now?" She screeched.

Desirae's breathing was ragged, and her eyes were wild. "You must come quickly, my Queen! It's Lucien; he has… he has…" her voice trailed off as she wrung her hands and glanced over her shoulder repeatedly.

She shed her body towel, allowing it to fall in a heap on the floor. She then grabbed her bathrobe off the hook by the door and donned it as she strode out of her room with the nanny leading the way. They both raced purposefully in the direction of Jax's quarters, Desirae on her heels.

When she arrived, she flung the door open and was immediately filled with horror.

Lucien was seated on the floor in his blue romper, which was covered in blood. Her cat, her Jax, had been sawn open by her own letter opener; the cat was in pieces, and her son was playing with its innards joyfully. She was immediately filled with fright, disgust, and dismay. Blood rushed into her head, and it seemed to be all she could hear in her head. Spots filled her vision, and it took all of her strength to remain on her feet.

"Lucien…" she began, her voice weak from vertigo.

The boy turned to her, his eyes alight with a fire from within. His smile was broad and satisfied, and he said to her, "See, mama, I play with Jax." He giggled hysterically and threw a handful of blood and tissue into the air before looking back at her to take in her reaction; he was reveling in his mother's confusion and pain.

Rasia's eyes rolled back into her head, and everything turned black as she hit the floor in a full faint.

"Ha, ha!" Lucien laughed as he continued to play with the feline's corpse. He turned to Desirae. "Mama shared Jax with me!"

R.W.K. Clark

CHAPTER 3

Patrick Gilliam sat in his den at his home. His elbows rested on his desk, and his fingers were steepled beneath his chin, supporting his head. He was deep in thought about his life. He could not believe all that had taken place since the fateful diving trip to Honduras with his friends. It all seemed almost unreal now.

So much had happened to bring about the changes in his life since he and his three friends had found the underwater cave. The Master, Cyril DeSai, rest his soul, has given him life eternal. The only thing he had felt missing was true love, and he found her almost immediately.

His Rose. How beautiful she was, and she was innocent. From the moment they met, he had determined to keep her from his own anguished fate: living eternally. It was not natural, and though he loved and appreciated DeSai for the gift, he wanted Rose to remain untainted by the curse.

So he protected her, keeping her hidden under lock and key. She was aware fully of what he was, and she loved him enough to trust his desire for her life. She submitted to him in every way, including allowing him to hunt when the need overtook him.

Yes, that was real love, and in return, he would keep her from the same fate for as long as possible. No one knew about her; he allowed no one in their home ever. When she became pregnant, he learned all he could learn about pregnancy and childbirth, caring for her himself, and even delivering their daughter.

Ah, the breathtaking Isabella Scarlet, his gorgeous, perfect offspring. Not yet two, she was more intelligent and beautiful than both of her parents. Yes, she was both human and vampire, but as of yet, she had shown no signs of the darker half taking charge. It seemed to Patrick that he and Rose had gotten the best of both worlds in their daughter, the perfect balance. She was playful, creative, imaginative, and kind.

Patrick did take Isabella out among the Family; Rose understood that it had to be this way. When they would question her existence, in the beginning, he simply explained it away by telling others that her mother left in the night. They did not question him. After all, Patrick had been the very first among them all to be bitten; he was considered royalty to a degree. Being the first human to have been turned by Master DeSai made him a celebrity among Family members, but he handled the adoration and the responsibility that came with it, with grace and dignity, just as the Master would have expected.

There was a slight tapping at his door. "Yes?" he asked, and the door opened slowly. Rose stood there smiling, her silky blond waist-length hair shining in the light of his lamp.

"Come," he said, smiling at his wife. "How has your day been?"

Rose entered the office and closed the door softly behind her. "Good," she replied. "Isabella is asleep for the night, so I came to see you." She beamed when she looked at him. Rose worshipped him, as he did her.

Then he remembered the dream he had the night before, and it caused his smile to fade. The Powers wanted Isabella for their own, and they had made that clear in his sleeping vision. She had been chosen to be married to Lucien, the Master's son, the one born to the Queen, Rasia. The thought turned his stomach. He knew there was no escaping this fate for Isabella; there was nothing he could do.

Patrick motioned for Rose to come to him. She came around his desk and sat on his lap, wrapping her arms around his neck and kissing his forehead as she did. "Are you okay, my love? You seem distracted."

"Yes, yes, I'm fine," he replied. "I couldn't be happier."

They held each other in silence for a while, Patrick rocking his desk chair back and forth. He would have to tell her. She would be heartbroken but, as always, she would understand. When would the time be right?

"Patrick, I need to talk to you," Rose said.

He looked at her, his eyes smiling. "Tell me."

Rose's smile faltered for a moment before she continued. "Patrick, I think I am very sick."

Immediately his stomach sank. This was something

he had always feared, losing his wife to her own mortality. "Why do you say this, Rose?"

She cleared her throat and looked down at her lap. "You know the cough I have had as of late?"

"Yes," Patrick said.

She continued to look down. "I have been coughing up quite a bit of blood."

As soon as she said it, he knew. She had been coughing all the time lately, and her already pale skin had become even more ashen than normal. Also, the most distressing point was that he could smell something coming from her; he could smell the sickness inside of her.

Taking her to a doctor would not do; it would give his family away, and she would become a feast for the one true Family. The only option he could think of was unthinkable: he would bite her, even though this concerned him as well. A bite was known to go both ways; it could give her life eternal, or it would progress her sickness, killing her with great speed.

He was willing to take the risk, but he needed to think about it for a while. "Rose, I will consider this deeply for a day or two. I will find a suitable solution, so I do not want you to fret. Are you worn out too badly?"

"No," she replied. "The cough and the blood are the only symptoms, but they are getting worse."

Patrick nodded as he gazed at her with a blinding love. "Give me a short time. I will solve the problem."

Rose smiled at him and kissed him on the mouth. "Of course, dear," she said, even though she had her doubts. "I'm going to turn in. Isabella wore me out today."

They embraced each other once more before Rose left him. When the door was securely closed behind her, he sat back in his chair and closed his eyes and spoke, saying, "Show me the way…"

It would all work out for the best.

It had to.

∞

Rasia sat at her desk in her office, the Book open in front of her. She was not reading it, though; she was simply trying to get her mind off her demonic son, but she found that even the Book's sacred ancient pages could do nothing to help her. All she could think about was clumps of black, bloody fur that covered her son and the floor around him.

Lucien. Oh, he was eviler than she had ever imagined he could be. The boy was not yet two years of age, and already he wanted to maim and mangle. He seemed to be filled with this dark spirit! Not only that, he seemed to thoroughly enjoy carrying out his violent desires.

But what did she expect? The boy was the offspring of a vampire and a witch, the first and only one of his kind. The potential for blackness in his soul was immeasurable. She sighed heavily and closed the Book, then locked it safely away. She had no idea what to do, and the Powers were silent when she went to them for answers.

After she discovered what Lucien had done to her

cat, she had been physically ill for hours. Desirae had taken the boy and cleaned him up, putting him down for a nap before cleaning up the mess in the cat's quarters, but Rasia had locked herself in her room, vomiting intermittently as pictures of the gruesome scene flashed through her mind.

She knew he would have intelligence, and she knew he would be powerful, at least in the end, but she had no comprehension of how dark he would be from the very start. Even before he crawled, he had a look in his eyes that betrayed his intelligence and black soul; he had just been powerless to carry anything out. It frightened her beyond any fear she had ever felt before. He looked at her with hatred, if that were possible for a toddler. Did he hate her because it was his nature or because he knew her thoughts and cravings toward him? Yes, she craved his blood, and yes, she despised his very existence, but he couldn't possibly know about either of those things.

Or did he?

Was that what fed the fuel of his hatred toward her? He had no other reason to despise her so. She grew tired of her pondering and shook the thoughts violently from her head. He was controlling far too much of her life! It would stop, and she would stop it. One way or another it would come to an end, or she would not make it even half-way through the boy's childhood without defying the Powers and making dinner out of her own son.

She made her way to her sanctuary, where a marble pentagram and altar waited for her continually. She stripped of her clothing and began to dance around the circle, chanting for the Powers once again to give her wisdom and insight. She also asked for permission, for the hundredth time, to end the life of Lucien Cerebus DeSai.

As she danced, her knees became weak, and suddenly she was thrown violently to the floor by an unseen force. She landed directly in the center of the pentagram, and her head bounced off the floor. Immediately she raised her hands to the spot on her head and began to rub it, and as she did, a dark cloud filled the air over her body; it was almost like a cloud of black smoke, and it even reeked of brimstone.

"Rasia DeSai, kneel before me!" The voice was a deep growl without any real tone, but Rasia could sense the pulsating fury in the monotone voice. The Powers were very, very angry with her.

She continued to hold her head as she struggled to get to her knees. When she did, she tried to look up at the smoke, but it scolded her. "You are not worthy to gaze upon me! Look down!"

She obeyed immediately. She had never experienced a visual or audible manifestation of the Powers; all of her responses from them had been in an emotional sense, and she was petrified. Rasia trembled, and her eyes fluttered in fear. Surely she had enraged them, and she would not push her luck any further by disregarding direct verbal orders.

"You have been chosen to be the mother of our son, and you will submit," the voice continued. "Who are you, who have been gifted with all things, to question us in any way? You are but our slave…"

Tears began to escape from her eyes, but she remained still as the voice continued. "If the boy Lucien killed you and feasted on your flesh tomorrow, it would be our will. You will get your senses about you and continue with the task you have been given. You were not born for your own pleasure, but to carry out the tasks which we desire."

Rasia squeezed her eyes tightly, and her tears dropped to the floor. "The pathetic water leaking from your eyes tastes wonderful," the voice purred. "Perhaps we will be pleased to harm you more another time. For now, you will mother the boy Lucien, and you will guide him properly, for one day he will rule over not only the world but you as well."

Rasia only nodded in agreement as the Powers continued. "As for you, you will never again come into our presence whining like a child, or you will be put to death and the child raised by another of our choosing," it said. "Bring a sacrifice to show remorse for your weakness. That will be your task for tomorrow evening. By the way, Rasia, your cat was delicious."

The cloud suddenly disappeared as quickly as it had come, and Rasia collapsed to the floor sobbing. Had Lucien sacrificed Jax to the Powers? No, she thought not. He had no knowledge of them, but if they freely incited him to do such, he would have obeyed. He was born with a heart for them.

She blew out the candles and switched on the dim light in the sanctuary. As she dressed, she got her tears under control, then she made her way back to her room, still rubbing the lump that had formed on her head. There she cleaned her face and brushed her hair before climbing into her bed.

"Oh, Cyril!" she said as she lay on her pillow. "How I regret taking your life! If ever I have felt pain and loneliness, it is now."

Rasia buried her face in her pillow and cried herself to sleep. She was trapped, just as she had intended to trap Cyril over two long years ago.

R.W.K. Clark

CHAPTER 4

"Rose, when you get Isabella to sleep, would you come to my office, darling?" Patrick had poked his head into their daughter's room.

Rose smiled at him. "Do you want me to come now?" she asked.

"No, dear. Make sure the little beauty is asleep though before you come." He shut the door gently and went to his den to wait for his wife to arrive.

Patrick sat at his desk as he waited, thinking about his conference with the Powers the night before. It had gone much better than anticipated; the Powers knowing that she would mother the chosen bride of the future Master, Patrick went imploring that the Powers provide an acceptable solution that would grant Rose her very life.

He had given them the best thing he could find for a sacrifice: an innocent sheep. They had reveled in its blood, and when he asked for their guidance, they were happy to give it to him. Yes, he should bestow her with the bite. No, her illness would not progress to the point of death from it. Rose was needed to raise an acceptable bride; she was chosen by the Powers long ago to birth and raise Isabella properly. They informed him that the child Isabella was very special indeed, though they did not give Patrick any details that mattered.

So, now, Patrick would tell Rose of the verdict, and he would help her make herself ready for the massive step she was about to take, but only if she was fully willing. If he sensed any apprehension in her at all, he would refuse to go through with it. The thought of her refusing the gift petrified him to no end.

A full half-hour passed before he heard Rose's gentle knock on his door. It pulled him out of his deep reverie, and he bid her entry. She took her normal seat across the desk from him, coughing softly into a tissue as she looked at him imploringly.

"Rose, I have come to a solution, one of which I'm sure you have anticipated," he began. "The only thing needed will be your whole-hearted agreement and willingness. Otherwise, I will not proceed."

She cleared her throat and smiled at him. "Of course, and yes, I know what it is. I must let you bite me."

Patrick held her eyes as he sat back in his chair. "I need you to understand, fully, exactly what that means." With that, Patrick spent the next hour explaining in great detail all the points that surrounded what they were about to do. It was so much more than eternal life. It was dark emptiness for all time.

At the end of his confessions, Rose smiled at him. "I understand, and I am willing. I love you, Patrick, and I love our Isabella. I must remain here, and I fear that without remedy I will soon be gone. Very soon."

Patrick looked his wife over carefully. Yes, she was pale, and her body was constantly wracked with coughing fits that caused her body obvious pain. As he gazed at her even now, he realized how thin and sickly she had really become, and the reality of her physical state hit him hard.

Now the two sat in silence, the air around them filled with electric anticipation. To Patrick, the bite meant that Rose would be with him eternally, and he was so relieved. He sensed no apprehension, no doubt. Yes, he would proceed.

"We will meet tonight in the bedroom," he told her. "All must be just right."

Rose nodded and smiled as she stood to her feet. She walked around his desk and, placing her hand on his back, kissed him with great love. She then looked him in the eyes. "I will be ready. I am more than ready, love. Please, do not worry that you will be doing me an injustice. The truth is you are giving me the gift of life, with both you and our beautiful Isabella."

With that Rose left the den. Patrick Gilliam tossed things around in his mind for only a moment before he buried his head in his hands. He had committed so much time and effort to avoid this, but it was obviously time.

Patrick had only one true desire for Rose: that she remain pure and untainted by the emptiness and pain that accompanied life after being bitten. She was so lovely, both inside and out, and he didn't want her to become anything less. To be a vampire, in Patrick's personal opinion, was to be less.

Finally, he stood and dried his face with a handkerchief. He would need to be strong. There was a plan in place, and he and his family were an integral part of it.

∞

Rasia lay in bed, the sun streaming through the window. It did not cast its rays on her, rather it simply lent light to the room. She was feeling that powerful lust, and it seemed to be consuming her. All she could think about was ravishing the flesh of a man; it had been two whole days! But there was no time for that now. Lucien would be having his breakfast and expecting her to get him started on his daily lessons. No, she could do nothing to quench this sexual thirst right now, but she would definitely indulge herself tonight.

She rose and took a quick hot shower to wash the filth of her sleep off of her body, then she dressed and did a light makeup on her face. Finally, she left her room with her small copies of the books which served as Lucien's study texts. He would be done eating now, and he would be angry if he had to wait too long for her to appear.

As he had aged, the boy had become more and more demanding. For a child of only four, he seemed to know perfectly what he wanted, and he expected her full cooperation. He did not fight her off when it came to things like his lessons. It was as if he had enough wisdom to know that they were necessary.

He excelled at them. It was spectacular to observe him learning. He had already mastered reading; he was easily as good a reader as any high school student would have been. His math skills were at a fourth-grade level, and he showed an understanding of history and science that was nothing short of frightening.

In the world that existed before, he would have been considered a child prodigy. But Rasia knew the truth; her son Lucien was nothing less than a spawn of hell, and whatever purpose he had been born to fulfill required his superior intelligence. It was all the work of the Powers.

She also knew that, at his age and size, he was not yet strong enough to take her life. If he tried, Rasia was sure that the Powers would not yet allow it. She realized that she had used the word 'yet' in her thoughts, and it was very unsettling. It was as though she knew deep inside that someday the boy would be her demise, perhaps taking her very life himself.

Rasia entered the chamber that served as Lucien's school room, and as she suspected, the boy was at his desk, working away.

"Good morning, my dear," she began, hiding the timidity that threatened to show itself through her voice.

Lucien did not even look up from his studies. "You are late, Mother."

Rasia raised her eyebrows. The boy's boldness never ceased to amaze her. "Yes, Lucien, and that would be none of your business, now would it?"

He turned to her, his eyes filled with fire, and in a firm voice stated. "It is all my business, you know that."

A chill ran down Rasia's spine.

She chose to ignore him and took her place at her desk, which was situated facing his. As she set her books down, she kept her eyes firmly on his face. He was, indeed, a beautiful child. She wondered to herself how such a small, handsome body could contain such evil. It seemed to be at a level far beyond his years, a level which is usually only demonstrated by one who has been a victim of life's cruel jokes.

"What are you working on?" she asked him as she made herself comfortable in her chair.

Without looking up, Lucien said, "I am beginning the new chapter in my mathematics book."

"But Lucien, you have not tested for the last chapter," Rasia told him, anger and impatience creeping into her voice. He knew better than to ever move on without her!

Keeping his eyes on his notebook, he plucked another sheet out from under it and tossed it carelessly in her direction. It see-sawed on the air for only a moment before coming to rest before her. He then looked up at her with a sneer before turning his attention back to his work.

Rasia looked down at the sheet. It was the test she had made up for the last chapter, the test he would have taken with her today, had he waited. It was completed in full very neatly, almost sarcastically so. She picked it up and looked at Lucien.

"Where did you get this?" she asked.

He continued to pencil away at his paper. "From the folder with all the math tests in them. The one in the second drawer on the right."

"Lucien, you are never to get into my desk! We have had this rule since the very beg—," she began, her voice progressively rising to a fever pitch as her impatience with the boy grew.

He cut her off. "Just check it, please. I am ready to do the new chapter, so just check it."

Rasia could only stare at the youngster in frustration. Oh, how she longed for Cyril to be here so he could help her with this unruly boy! How could a four-year-old child be so infuriating, so demanding? She set the test paper down on her desk with a sigh and took out her own answer sheet. She would correct the paper.

As she began, she found herself hoping that she would find a number of mistakes, but to her surprise the test was perfect.

"Lucien, put your pencil down and look at me," she said.

The child raised his pencil from the paper, but he did not look at her for a long moment. Finally, his gaze met hers, and his eyes were filled with anger. It took her a moment to pull herself together so she could speak to him with a tone of authority.

"Did you also take my answer key and copy the answers?"

Lucien threw his pencil onto his desk with force, causing it to bounce off the surface onto the floor.

"You think I cheated?" he asked her with great anger in his voice.

"I am simply asking you," she replied.

The small boy growled. "I will take it again, in front of you, if you like." How dare this woman challenge him!

"I'll tell you what, Lucien. You continue with what you are doing for the time being. I will make up a new test, and you will take that one, and yes, you will take it in front of me," she told him through clenched teeth.

The two stared each other down for a short moment before the boy rose and retrieved his pencil from the floor. He resigned himself to his fate, mumbling to himself as he sat back down and turned his attention to the new chapter.

As Rasia made up his new test, she boiled with anger. The child thought himself her equal! Worse yet, he seemed to know how far 'above' her he truly was, and he didn't mind throwing it in her face with great pleasure. How dare he presume to get into her desk, steal her test sheet, and take the test unsupervised? She proceeded to make up terribly hard test questions for a four-year-old child, but she knew deep in her soul that he would ace the new test as well. She was fully aware that she was only doing this to show the boy who was really boss, and it disgusted her that she had such little control over her own offspring. Why did he force her to go to such lengths?

Within twenty minutes, she had finished making up the new test, and she had Lucien begin it immediately.

He took it from her with no emotion, and as he completed the problems she had given him, she stared at him. After only fifteen minutes, the boy tossed the paper at her in a replay of his earlier gesture of disrespect. Rasia did not let it get under her skin; she simply began to check the problems and his work.

In five minutes she was finished. He got the entire test correct, and she was at a loss for words. His intelligence was growing faster than she could keep up with it. She looked up at the small boy without saying anything. He was toiling away at the problems in the new chapter. Suddenly he spoke to her without looking up.

"Are you happy now, Mother?"

∞

That evening, Rasia put the boy down early. He had given her horrible attitude all day, and she needed to relieve her stress. When she had laid him down, she had attempted to smooth things over by sitting on the side of his bed and reading a story to him, but the scent of the blood coursing through his veins was as strong as a steak being cooked on hot coals. It made her squirm the entire time, and she practically had to run from the room to keep herself from biting him.

Rasia sat thinking for only a minute; she wanted her Book. It was the only thing that truly fulfilled her, as it was a sharp, steady reminder of her sole purpose in the world. She was here for only one thing: to carry out the bidding of the Powers.

She went to her room and got the Book from the

safe in her desk. What spell shall I work tonight? She asked herself this as she prepared for Lamb to bring her next victim.

She had nothing to ask the Powers for; all was hers. She had adoration: on Earth, she was a goddess. She had a 'family' if you could call all these servants such.

The only thing left was for Rasia to continue to feed the unsettled sexual desire which demanded to be fulfilled every minute of every day. She considered this unquenchable fire between her legs; she did not understand it. Why could she not stop thinking about being licked and serviced? It was all she seemed to think about.

Tonight she will treat herself. She had been filled with unbearable desire for too long, and now she would indulge her own lusts.

Rasia bathed and perfumed herself, applying a light makeup as well. She donned a flowing satin gown and made herself comfortable on her bed, waiting for Martin to arrive with her treat. She could barely contain herself. Oh, the things she would make him do when he arrived…

She didn't have to wait too long. A knock on her door brought her out of her mental fantasy, and she bid the caller to enter. A young man of about twenty-six entered her room, closing the door behind him.

"Make sure you lock it," she told him. "It will not do to have my son wandering in here."

He locked the door and then turned to her. "What can I do for you tonight, my Queen?"

Rasia stood and walked slowly toward him, taking in the sight of him. He was quite beautiful, with his perfect brown hair and brown eyes. His features seemed almost chiseled, and his muscled body strained against the material of his button-down shirt.

"Well, for starters, it would be ideal if you did not speak," she told him calmly.

She circled him not once, but twice. Then she stood directly in front of him, looking him in the eye. She reached out and pulled his shirt from his jeans and began to unbutton it. Then she violently pressed her lips against his, invading his mouth with her tongue. He responded passionately; she could almost feel his admiration and... love, but she didn't care. His purpose was strictly utilitarian.

Rasia pulled away from him. "Take your clothes off," she said. She removed her own gown, then stood before him and gazed at his nakedness. Yes, he would do.

Now she approached him once again and took him by the hand. She led him to her bed and positioned herself on it, kneeling and facing him. He was smiling at her, but she was not smiling back.

"Lie down," she said simply.

He made himself comfortable on his back, gazing up at her. He was completely erect, his penis nearly standing upright. She looked at it only for a moment before straddling his face.

"Taste me," she demanded, and he willingly dove in.

For the next twenty minutes, she ground herself

against his nose, mouth, and tongue. She came not once, not twice, but three times, before she pulled away and forcefully sat upon his rock-hard member. The pain and pleasure it gave her were exquisite, and she moaned loudly as she rode him.

She climaxed the final time powerfully, her entire body stiffening on his. He had his hands on her hips and was forcing himself deeper inside her. Even in her orgasmic reverie, she knew he was about to cum, and she would have none of it. The last thing she wanted was any of him… left inside of her.

She looked down at him as he strained to climax. His eyes fluttered open, and a smile crossed his lips when suddenly she swooped down on him and bit into his neck. She tore the flesh away violently, and his blood spurted out, going airborne and splattering across the canopy of her bed. Rasia simply remained on top of him, feeling his erection disappear inside of her. His flesh and part of his jugular vein dangled from her bloody mouth, and she watched the life flow out of him.

Yes, she thought to herself. That was quite extraordinary.

Yes, it was enjoyable when it was happening, the sex, but when it was over, she was filled with such an unbearable disgust with the one she had used that she could not even bear to look at them. Initially, she had thought that perhaps she could find love with another, but with each sexual escapade that hope faded. She would never know love again, not like the love she had felt for Cyril. That was her own personal hell, to have tasted it and then have it taken from her for all eternity.

Rasia rose off of him and sat on the edge of the bed. She took the telephone in her hand and dialed Martin Lamb's extension. He answered with a sleepy voice.

"Get up here and get this mess cleaned up," she directed. "Oh, and Martin? Keep it quiet."

∞

Lucien lay still in his bed in the darkness. He could see very well in the dark, so it never did bother him to have the lights out; in fact, he always preferred it. His mother had left him more than two hours ago, believing that he was sleeping, but he had not slept a wink. The truth was, he really didn't need that much rest.

He listened carefully in the darkness to the noises coming from different areas of the house. He had very good ears, and there was very little that went on in the massive house that he did not take in. There were late night noises of preparations being made in the kitchen for tomorrow's meals. He could even hear Martin Lamb's lips move in silence as he read some nonsense book. Now he was listening to the panting and moaning and groaning that could only be coming from his mother's room.

How he hated his Mama! She thought she knew so much and he knew so little, and maybe that was true, but he did know that she was not as important as he. Even she was not fully aware of this fact. She seemed to think that, no matter what, she would always be a step above him because of her age and her strength. He knew she hated him too, but he did not care.

She looked at him often as if he were dinner, and it made him uncomfortable. He did not understand the look in her eye when she did this, but it put him on the defense always. He believed that if he did not show her who was boss, she would try to... eat him. Sometimes she even smelled him. She did not realize that he noticed, but he did notice, and he was determined to take her down before she ever had a real chance to hurt him.

He listened as the sound of his mother's moaning grew yet again, then he heard her hushed voice say something jumbled, and he could not quite make it out. After that, the entire house seemed to grow deathly quiet.

Lucien smiled. Another visitor, gone.

There was a definite pattern to the noises he heard from her room and the silence that followed, but at his age, Lucien was not quite sure what it was. They came, they caused chaos, and then they were gone, but even Lucien knew there was something more to the entire procession.

Well, if any of them knew Mama like he did, they would never have come here in the first place. Whatever she did to them was their own fault. Something wasn't right with her, and in his mind this fact was obvious. No, something was very wrong.

But something was off about himself, and he knew that too. The thought made the young boy's smile grow in the darkness.

After all, what was really 'right,' and what was 'wrong'? Who was to say?

His smile suddenly faded as he reminded himself that someone determined right from wrong, but he did not 'know' that someone.

Not yet, anyway.

The silence from Mama's room persisted, and Lucien grew bored with listening.

Finally, he turned over on his side and fell into a deep, content sleep. Tomorrow would bring more opportunities for him to annoy the witch, and he looked forward to it with gusto.

R.W.K. Clark

CHAPTER 5

Everything went according to plan for Patrick and Rose Gilliam.

The night he turned his wife was perfect. They made love by firelight, and when he bit her, he instantly knew he had no worries; she was going to be fine. Rose immediately reveled in the healing effect the bite had on her health.

Over the next few months, she came into her own, vampire-wise. She filled the shoes beautifully, and Patrick couldn't be more pleased. Rose seemed to grow in grace if that were at all possible, and she did not seem to grow in evil as Patrick had worried she would. They would raise Isabella together and be with her for all eternity. He looked back on the night and all of its details with great fondness. It had been the night all of his stress and care regarding his wife, and their future together left him for good.

∞

Now Isabella was four years old, and even though she was half human, she showed the sharpness and intelligence of her vampire heritage with great power. Both Patrick and Rose were very, very proud parents indeed. The girl showed great promise, and they knew that the Powers were pleased, both with her existence and the contributions that they both made to it.

She was also strikingly beautiful, even for such a young child. She had long, silky blond hair and eyes the color of rich, sparkling sapphire. Her eyelashes were so long and lush that they threatened to tangle together when she blinked. She was a very attractive young girl indeed, and her catering parents loved to contemplate how breathtaking she would be when she was fully mature.

One of their favorite things to do with Isabella was to take her to the large park only a mile from their home. They would let her play for hours on the toys there, and the girl adored going. It was on one of these trips that the family made the acquaintance of the Master's queen, Rasia DeSai.

The entire family was familiar with Rasia's existence and rule, but not all had come to meet her personally. As the matriarch of the Family, Rasia had a lot of responsibilities, not to mention a son of her own. No one had ever seen him, either, but they all celebrated his existence. He would one day master them all and rule the world.

The world they lived in was a beautiful place. There was no crime anymore because there was no law. They all shared everything, give and take. It was perfect on Earth, and the memory of the world as it was before was like a poor impression of a bad dream in the minds of everyone. The Family accepted the changes that had taken place, embracing all aspects of 'turning' with open arms and hearts. It was the selfishness of human nature which permitted them all to do so heartily.

∞

Patrick and Rose stood on either side of Isabella as they walked into the park area, holding her hands and swinging the child back and forth. She laughed with giddiness, tickled each time her feet left the ground. It was a beautiful day, and they would all enjoy their time here together.

As soon as Isabella saw the playground equipment, she began to twist her tiny hands in an effort to escape her parents. "Mommy, daddy, let go! I want to play!"

"Go!" Patrick shouted with love. The couple laughed and released their daughter, who ran with all of her might to get to the toys. Patrick looked at his wife and smiled; things could not be more perfect. He would not trade his life for anything.

They took a seat on a bench that was situated facing the playground. Rose snuggled against her husband, who draped his arm over her shoulders. They watched Isabella, smiles of love glued to their faces. She was completely intent on all of her climbing and sliding; it was as if she were all alone, without her parents, thriving in the atmosphere at the playground.

They were only at the park for about ten minutes when a young boy with longer raven-colored hair ran past them toward the playground equipment, startling both of them. They turned to see if he had supervision following him. A woman was rapidly approaching, though she seemed to take no notice of their presence on the bench.

"Lucien, slow down please," she shouted after the tot.

But the youngster paid no attention. Instead, he made a beeline for Isabella.

∞

"Hello," he stated simply, looking up at her as she dangled by her knees from one of the gymnastic bars on the playground.

She looked at him, her long blond hair nearly touching the ground. "Hi," she replied. "Wanna play with me?"

The boy Lucien wrapped his arm around one of the supporting poles on the playground equipment and kicked aimlessly at a rock on the ground; for some reason he suddenly felt very shy. "My name is Lucien. What's yours?"

"Isabella. Didn't you hear me? I asked you if you wanna play." The boy nodded, and with that Isabella did a flip and landed perfectly on her little feet on the ground, exhibiting all the grace of a seasoned feline.

Lucien's eyes grew wide. "Cool! How did you learn that?"

"I don't know," Isabella replied. "I never did it before." The two smiled at each other and ran off to climb the steps leading to the slide.

"Well, they seemed to hit it off," said Rasia as she neared the bench. Patrick and Rose nodded and smiled in agreement.

After a moment, Rose spoke. "I am Rose Gilliam, and this is my husband, Patrick. Our daughter there is Isabella."

The woman, who had long red hair and striking green eyes smiled tightly. "I am Rasia."

Now the smiles left their faces, and they were suddenly serious. "Our Queen," Patrick began. "I am so sorry. I did not recognize you." Both Patrick and Rose stood immediately to demonstrate respect for their queen.

Rasia smiled tightly at them and nodded. "Please, sit. Don't concern yourselves," she replied. "Lucien and I do not often venture out, but today he was not content to play in the courtyard. Let us be parents together today."

Patrick and Rose sat back down, and the three adults sat in silence, watching the children take turns on the slide, each laughing hysterically with each trip down. After only a few turns apiece, they made their way to the swings, walking and talking, though their tones were low and hushed.

Rasia watched the interaction closely, though Isabella's parents did not seem at all concerned. The kids continued to giggle and whisper to each other. Then Lucien turned to Rasia and smiled with satisfaction. The hair on the back of Rasia's neck stood up. He always seemed to know something she did not, and it was infuriating to her that the Powers seemed to trust a young boy more than they did her.

He reached down and took Isabella's hand, then they began to walk to the swings, clenching their hands together, their parents forgotten behind them.

CHAPTER 6

"Lucien, are you coming to my house for my birthday dinner?" Isabella and Lucien were in the family room at the White House playing video games. The two had become instant best friends, and now three years had already passed.

Isabella was already in a sort of childlike love with Lucien. In her mind, she would marry him someday, and of this, she had no doubt. Sometimes her nearly seven-year-old mind would fantasize for hours about their wedding and all of its details. She would go through her mother's magazines and fantasize about wedding cakes and dresses. She knew it would be just perfect when the day came.

"Of course I will," he replied. "Now hush. You are only trying to talk to me because you are losing."

This made Isabella laugh so hard she dropped her game controller and nearly fell out of her seat. "You always figure me out," she told him.

Suddenly the door opened, and Patrick entered. "Isabella, it's time to go. We have a lot to do at home to prepare for tomorrow." She would have family time during the day to celebrate her birthday, but the dinner with Lucien and his mom were what Isabella was truly looking forward to.

The girl stood and groaned. "Do I have to go? Can't you and mom take care of it?"

"Isabella, we have talked about this. We do these things together," her father told her in a calm, controlled tone that meant business.

She kicked at the carpet. "Ugh," she said. "Lucien, I have to go."

Now Lucien turned his attention from the game, even going so far as to put down his controller without pausing it. "Mr. Gilliam, surely you can make an exception."

Patrick looked at Lucien. The boy had made him a bit nervous ever since he had first gotten to know him, and this was a feeling that had not lessened over time. "Lucien, her mother and I have made plans for tonight that include Isabella."

Now Lucien stood and walked up to him calmly and looked up at him, making sure they made direct eye contact. "Don't be such a bastard, Patrick."

Patrick's flesh broke out in goosebumps. This child was straight from hell. "Lucien, I don't appreciate how you spoke to me. Do you not have any respect?" He turned to his daughter. "Isabella, come now!"

The girl darted for her father, not because she wanted to, but because he was her father. Patrick took her by the hand and began to back out the door. "Lucien, I don't know that I even want you to come for dinner tomorrow unless you change your attitude and start behaving with respect."

Lucien just looked at the man and smiled. He shifted his gaze momentarily toward Isabella, they looked back at Patrick. "Of course, Mr. Gilliam, you are right. I apologize, and I will be at dinner tomorrow."

Patrick continued to look the boy in the eyes; he didn't mean a word of what he said, Patrick knew with surety. He was simply fixing things for the sake of Isabella. Rather than challenge the boy's apology though, he simply nodded and left the room with the girl, who dragged unenthusiastically after him.

Once the door was closed, Lucien opened his mouth and let out a blood-curdling scream that was accompanied by a growl that seemed to come from some unseen beast. He turned and kicked his game console, then picked the unit up and smashed it against the wall. He then ran over to the bookcase next to the television and turned it face down, spilling all the books to the floor. Finally, he pushed the television itself face-first to the floor, smashing its screen to bits.

Rasia ran into the room as Lucien tried to catch his breath. She was stunned as she looked around at the destruction this small seven-year-old boy had managed to dole out on the room.

Finally, she spoke to him quietly. "Lucien, go to your room. I will be up to speak with you in a short while."

He looked and her and clenched his teeth. Then he balled his fists. "I will go, but know I would have rather done this to you and your pathetic friends," he said.

"Consider yourself lucky." He then rushed past her and ran down the hall toward the stairs.

Rasia turned her attention back to the room. For the love of the Powers, the small child had turned the place upside down! Patrick had told her what Lucien had said to him, and she had been heading in to confront him, only to discover his violent behavior. With each passing day, her fear of her son grew stronger; she had no idea how to take any next step with him without the Powers providing her with wisdom and strength. She would certainly fail at raising this boy without the guidance they provided her with.

She made her way back to the dining room where she had been having coffee with the Gilliams and Desirae, the nanny, before the incident between Lucien and Patrick. "Desirae, I need you to have Ronald clean up the family room," she said quietly. "Lucien has had some sort of… fit. Then I want you to go up and talk calmly to him. Find out what set him off, please. I'm sure he will not confide in me."

Desirae rose to do Rasia's bidding, leaving the room in a hurry. Rasia sat at her place at the head of the table and put her head in her hands. How could she properly raise the future ruler of this world when he despised her? The Powers had stopped giving her answers long ago; all they bestowed on her now for her sacrifices was the strength to survive him, and she was utterly and completely lost most of the time regarding the next proper step to take.

Well, she would give Desirae a few minutes with the

boy, and that time would also serve well for Rasia to calm down her emotions and gather a bit of courage to confront his actions herself.

He was only seven, but with each passing year, he grew cockier, and yes, more dark and determined. Patrick said the boy had used the word 'bastard' in reference to him. Rasia had never known Lucien to behave that way with other adults, particularly Isabella's own father or mother. It was a dark and depressing omen. She returned to the dining room to finish the rest of her coffee before going upstairs to deal with the boy.

∞

"Lucien, can I come in?" Desirae stood outside the boy's room and waited for a response.

After a momentary pause, she heard his voice come through the door. "Yeah, sure. Come on," he said.

Desirae turned the knob and entered the room. It was dark, the heavy curtains pulled and no lights on. She reached to her left and flipped the switch, flooding the room with sudden bright light. Lucien sat on the bed cross-legged, a look of dark rage over his face. Desirae was at once uneasy.

She cleared her throat. "I know you are upset, Lucien, and I just wondered if I could do anything?"

He continued to look at her in silence, only shaking his head in response.

She approached him slowly and sat on the very edge of the bed at its foot. "What happened?" she asked softly, her hands trembling slightly. Lucien noticed, and it amused him.

The boy turned to her. "I am tired of all of you grown-ups," he said. "I don't know how, but someday I will make all of you pay."

Desirae took in a sharp breath. She was very familiar with Lucien and his erratic behavior, but it never ceased to shock her. This was the son of the deceased Master? She found it very hard to believe, as the Master was never so evil and disrespectful to those around him. He showed great love and care to the members of his Family.

She continued to look at the boy carefully. He was a mass of tension, and his eyes were dark and brooding. He was sitting on his hands, and his own anger was driving him to rock back and forth. Suddenly the nanny was filled with compassion. The boy was only seven! Future leader or not, how did they all expect him to behave the way Rasia truly demanded? It was impossible.

Her wary gaze softened a bit. "I know how you feel," she began.

"Do you?" He turned to her, his eyes blazing, and Desirae thought for a fraction of a second that a grown man was seated before her.

Suddenly he pulled his right hand out from under his leg and swung it in her direction. She flinched, but what was happening barely had time to register in her mind. In a flash, the boy Lucien buried a pair of scissors in her throat so far that the tip of them came out the back of her neck.

Desirae froze, the injury rendering her motionless.

With wide eyes she stared at the boy, who sat smiling at her, watching as the blood poured out of the front of her neck, ran down his hand and arm, and finally pooled in one of the folds of her light jacket.

The last clear thought the nanny had was that her eye was twitching. She fell over on the bed, dead and lifeless. Lucien continued to watch the blood flow for a few minutes, his small hand still firmly grasping the scissors so he could feel her heartbeat until it finally stopped.

As if on cue, another knock came at the door, and before he could respond Rasia came in, and what she saw stole the breath from her lungs.

There was Lucien on his bed, calmly sitting and watching the bloody, lifeless body of Desirae as it lay there. It took a moment for the scene to become clear to Rasia, then she came to her senses and gasped for breath.

Maintaining as calm a demeanor as possible, Rasia spoke to her child, but she did not look at him; she continued to look at the lifeless body of the one-time nanny. "Lucien, go shower immediately. I need to clean this up," she told him with a still voice.

He rose and walked past her, and he smirked at her as he hit his elbow hard against her hip. Why not take the opportunity to cause the witch a bit of pain while he was at it? She ignored the intimidating act though, and once he was gone, she sighed aloud. "Oh, Desirae. I should have known better. I am so sorry." She pulled the blankets and sheets on her son's bed free of the mattress and wrapped them around the body, then she went to the hall phone and called Martin Lamb's extension.

"Martin, Lucien has made yet another mess," she said into the receiver. "I need help to clean it up."

As she put the receiver back on the cradle, she thought about Cyril once again. How would he have dealt with such exhibitions of violence from their son? She would never know, as she really didn't even know her husband that well. Rasia turned and went back into Lucien's room to wait for Martin, where the lifeless body of Desirae, blood-covered and pale, was waiting to be taken care of.

∞

Isabella and Lucien sat in the backyard of her home after her birthday dinner. They had eaten all the pizza they could stuff into themselves, along with chocolate cake and strawberry-vanilla ice cream. The girl felt so fat and satisfied that all she could do was smile and moan. Lucien was quietly doing the same.

The sun was beginning to go down, and the evening was beautiful. She felt satisfied that her friend had been able to come. "Lucien, where is Desirae?" she asked.

"She didn't feel good," he told her.

"Oh," she replied. "I thought that before we know it, we will be grown-ups, you know?"

He turned to her. "Yes, faster than we expect, I think."

Isabella's stomach fluttered. "I love you, Lucien. Do you love me?"

He looked off into the darkening sky. "Of course. You know I do."

"Someday I would like to be your wife," she said quietly. She could feel the blood rushing into her cheeks, and she was glad it was dark outside.

Lucien had taken hold of her hand in the dark, and now he squeezed it gently.

The poor, beautiful girl. Didn't she know he had no idea what love even was?

He turned to her. "We'll get married someday, so don't worry Isabella." He squeezed her hand again and looked back to the sky.

Isabella smiled and rested her head against the tree trunk, closing her eyes with quiet satisfaction. She felt happy and content.

She only wished that Desirae had been there for pizza; she really liked Desirae.

∞

Inside the house, Patrick, Rose, and Rasia sat huddled in the breakfast nook in the kitchen drinking glasses of Cabernet and talking in hushed tones.

"I tell you, I don't know what to do with him," Rasia was saying. "It seems he doesn't have a sane bone in his body, and this child is to rule the Family and the world? Oh, Cyril, I need you now!"

The Gilliams could see how terribly their queen was fretting. Yes, she was in a bind, that was for sure. Patrick and Rose were both acutely aware of the strange attitudes and behaviors Lucien demonstrated, but they weren't sure if it was all due to the darkness inside him or bad parenting on his mother's part. Patrick knew one thing for sure: if the Master had been here, the boy would have had the guidance he needed. Oh, well, it was a moot point now.

Rose patted Rasia's hand comfortingly. "It will be alright, Rasia. It is just his nature. As you have said, Lucien is the first of his kind."

"Yes," Patrick agreed. "The important thing for you to do is to continue to mother and nurture him. It is your responsibility, and we believe the Powers want it this way."

Rasia remained silent, turning her destiny over in her mind. The 'Powers,' Patrick had said. They knew the Powers that were really in charge. She was helpless, and she truly had no hope. The boy and his raising were her destiny.

∞

Once she was alone in her room at home, Rasia had time to relax. She had to do something to teach Lucien personal order; it was essential to an extent, as the leader of the Family. How would he ever properly lead the people of his father without any kind of wisdom or self-control? She knew he could not. Such behavior would only result in death and chaos, and she feared, with great trepidation, that her son would always be just out of her reach.

Once she had sent Lucien to bed, she changed into comfortable powder blue plaid pajamas; Rasia felt cold tonight and was anxious to slip beneath the covers of her bed and soak up the warmth that the darkness provided her with. She brushed her hair out and then did just that.

As she lay on her pillow, she thought of her child, the boy of destiny who had completely taken over her life. She wanted to cry, but no tears would come. It then occurred to her that she could not remember the last time she cried; had she ever cried at all?

She let a long sigh escape her lips. "Oh, Cyril. If only you knew how terribly I miss you and need you now. If only you were aware of the remorse, I feel for your death!"

She cried until her eyes became sore and heavy, but sleep did not come easily to Rasia, and when she did finally fall to slumber, she tossed and turned, tormented by evil dreams and monstrous visions which she could not recall upon waking. She knew now what the deep loneliness Cyril had described felt like, and this empty yearning, this incredible loneliness, was it.

Rasia woke off and on throughout the night, her personal stress robbing her of sleep. Her eyes, swollen from her tears, throbbed with heat, and each time she woke she found it harder and harder to return to her rest. She knew, with certainty, that this was all her life held for her now: emptiness, loneliness, confusion, and despair.

Oh, how she deserved it!

R.W.K. Clark

CHAPTER 7

Rasia had called a meeting the night after Isabella's own birthday dinner. The meeting included Mother, himself, and Mr. and Mrs. Gilliam.

Mother had initiated the meeting in their own family room. A cunning wench was she, Lucien thought.

"Lucien, have a seat," she began. "Are you thirsty, son? Do you need to use the bathroom?"

Lucien had glared at her. What the heck was going on?

Mother stopped toying with him then; she recognized the impatient, angry look on his face. He was not stupid, and there was no reason to play games with him. Her eyes caught fire, and she raised her voice, hardening it with authoritative tones. "Lucien, you killed Desirae the night before last," Rasia began.

Lucien glanced at the Gilliams and then looked back at his mother. "Yes, and?" He knew there was no reason to deny it; the three 'grown-ups' knew who he was, and they knew what he was.

"Very well," she said. "Beginning tonight, upon the very conclusion of this meeting, you will be escorted and guarded by a pair of male nurses at all times. These nurses have the authority to tranquilize you as needed, and they will be prepared to do so at all times."

"It is time you come to terms with your destiny," his mother continued her tirade harshly. "This is not what I would have liked to have either, Lucien, but it is what it is. You will come to learn order and delegation of authority, which includes self-control and wisdom, so you are able to properly lead the Family that your father has established. Do you understand what I am saying?"

The color had drained from his face. "I sincerely hope you're kidding."

"It is already done," she replied, struggling to keep her voice steady. She was afraid of how Lucien was going to react to the revelation she had just given him, but she was even more frightened by what he could become if the upper hand were not taken.

As soon as she said those words, the doors of the family room had opened, and two of the biggest guys he had ever seen had entered and taken him by his seven-year-old arms. He gave it all he had, kicking and screaming and squirming, but it had been useless. He felt a sharp sting in his upper arm, and that was the last thing he remembered.

When he had woken, he tried to go out into the hall once his head had cleared. The shot, the men had given him, had given him a headache, and his thoughts were also a bit clouded because of it, but he had a bone to pick with Mother. He sat on the edge of his bed for a short while, just until he began to feel a bit clearer, then he rose and walked to the door of his room to confront that witch who gave him birth.

But as soon as he had opened the door, the two guys were on him. He was too drained to fight or struggle much this time, and they weren't as rough with him as before. The light to his room came on with a flash, and he squinted in pain from the shock to his eyes.

The nurses put him on his bed and then stood back and watched him. They wanted to see how he would respond to them. He didn't have the energy to do anything other than ask them through clenched teeth, "Can I talk to my mother?"

The man closest to the door nodded. "I'll tell her you're awake." Then he was gone.

The second man took a syringe out of his breast pocket and removed the cap. He stood, ready and waiting, for Lucien to try anything.

"Ah, you're awake," his mother's voice broke through his steadily clearing haze. "Well, you have now properly met Roger and Carl, two of six nurses who will take shifts with you. Here are your choices, Lucien:

You can continue to behave in such an erratic and irresponsible manner that everyone fears for their lives constantly, in which case I will personally take extreme measures, to my very own peril with the Powers, or you can spend the next three years with these men, constantly." Rasia paused to let her words sink in.

After a moment of silence, she continued. "If you have demonstrated a desire to learn and gain a bit of much-needed discipline, you may be free of the burden on your tenth birthday. But until then, you are under their constant watch, and they are permitted to take matters into their own hands."

Lucien had turned all of this over in his head. He was seeing red; how he wanted this monstrosity of a witch to be dead. He felt frustrated and furious, but he did not show his fury.

"You are a very intelligent boy, beyond your years," she said. "Figure it out." With that Rasia turned sharply and left his room, slamming the door behind her.

The guard who had fetched his mother told him, "It's very late, you may as well use the bathroom and try to get some real sleep."

In a small show of defiance, Lucien met the nurse's gaze and slid back on his bed, supporting himself against the wall. He crossed his arms over his seven-year-old chest and looked away.

He had too many things to think about; he didn't have time to deal with them now.

∞

Lucien's tenth birthday would be a milestone for the boy, and he was excited. For the last three years, that witch of a mother of his had made him endure the company of two hulking male nurses. Ugh! Sure, he had managed to get his kicks in one way or another, but those two horse's asses had proven themselves to be a hindering annoyance.

∞

Now it was the morning of his tenth birthday, and as he lay in bed allowing his head to clear, his excitement grew. He had done it. He had made it an entire three years without killing all six of those bastards and his mother too.

His tenth birthday meant that his days with them were over.

He sat up quickly and jumped to the floor. He put on his robe and went to the bathroom to brush his teeth. Not only was he free, but birthdays usually always proved to be fun. He would get to eat as much as he wanted, and he got to spend the whole day with Isabella as well. Of all the people in his 'Family,' as Mother called it, Isabella was by far his favorite.

When he was finished in the bathroom, he ran downstairs and started looking for his mother. She was usually at the breakfast table in the nook off the dining room, but this morning the room was empty. Lucien wandered around their common living area, to no avail. When he entered the family room, he found Martin Lamb.

"Ah, good morning, Lucien, and happy birthday! Free of your annoying friends, I see," Martin said.

He didn't like Martin, but he was in too good a mood to let the man's unexpected presence ruin his day. "Yes. It's a relief. Where is my mother?"

"She had some things to pick up to prepare for the day," the man replied. "The Gilliams will be over to participate in the festivities with you both, as I am sure you are aware."

Lucien simply nodded in response and turned away, heading for the nook. He would eat alone, just as he had been doing for most of the last three years if he didn't count those smelly apes who had been his 'babysitters.' Mother had pretty much put a strong wedge between them both when it came to their personal relationship, but there was no love lost there for Lucien. He could care less, as long as the witch met his needs.

He took his regular seat at the table and rang the bell for breakfast to be brought to him. While he waited, he thought about the fact that he was sitting all alone in the house; it was almost overwhelming to him. At the beginning of his 'sentence,' he had daydreamed about ripping all of those musclemen apart with his bare hands and letting their blood drip through his fingers, but he knew that with two of them with him at a time, and both of them armed with drug-filled syringes, he didn't stand a chance. Even if he were successful in ridding himself of one of them, the other would get to him before he knew what was happening. The consequences would have been terrible for him.

So he had patiently bided his time without putting up even the slightest fight. After only eight months of good behavior, Mother had been impressed, but not enough to change the time frame in his favor. She didn't budge as far as his 'sentence' went.

The door to the kitchen opened and one of the servants brought him his breakfast of French toast and scrambled eggs, his favorite. Her hand trembled in fear as she set the plate down in front of him, and he took note of this with great amusement. But rather than allow her fear to whet his appetite, Lucien simply looked at the woman and smiled. "Thank you," he said sweetly to her.

She nodded in response, bowing slightly, and backed away toward the kitchen. He hadn't considered that the entire house would be filled with fear! This was going to be more fun than opening all the wrapped gifts in the world!

He wolfed his food down and was just drinking the last of his glass of milk when Mother entered the room. "Good morning, Lucien," she said cheerfully. "Eating alone, I see. How does it feel?"

Lucien immediately felt the hate building up in his stomach, working its way toward his throat. Oh, murdering this wench would be like having dessert, but he knew he needed to bide his time; he would get the job done someday, of that he was determined. He simply responded. "Awesome, Mother, thank you."

"Well, you will be free to do as you wish today, within reason, of course," Rasia began. "Isabella and her parents will be here around noon, and they will spend the remainder of the day here with us to help us celebrate. This is more than your tenth birthday to me, you know. You have shown great progress, Lucien."

He looked at her. Her eyes were filled with pride. It would take even more time than he thought to cut loose a bit, and he would have to be very careful and sneaky when indulging his own whims. Not to worry, Lucien, he told himself. Soon…

She turned away and left the room, and as soon as she was gone, he took the last bite of French toast, which sat on his plate, and wrapped it in his cloth napkin and placed it in the pocket of his robe. He smiled to himself with satisfaction. Then he began to consider his day.

He turned his mind to Isabella, his best good friend. He considered her his girlfriend in his mind, and even at his young age, he was sure they would be married someday. As a matter of fact, he was willing to bet that was the plan of their parents all along. He was okay with that; he could tell her anything, and she did not judge him or act like he was weird. He shared with her all of his temptations and desires, and she embraced them as a part of him.

He knew how Isabella felt about him, and while he had a certain affection for her, he wouldn't call it 'love.' She was a presence in his life that he knew was supposed to be there, and he honestly didn't know what he would do without her friendship. She was, after all, his best and only friend.

Lucien knew there was more to him than he understood. He also knew this about Isabella for that matter. They had talked about this amongst themselves in an effort to figure it all out. He believed it had something to do with the noises that came from his mother's room late at night on such a frequent basis. Sometimes the noises she made in there sounded more like she was an animal than a person. He just couldn't figure it out.

For the last three years, during his 'sentence,' he and Isabella had become closer than ever. Why just about a year ago she had let him kiss her for the very first time! He hadn't wanted to because of 'love,' he just wanted to know what it felt like, but after that kiss, Isabella changed toward him. She seemed to be a little more attached to him than before. He didn't mind. He considered her to be his and his alone.

Lucien made his way back up to his room, where he dressed in blue jeans, a t-shirt, and a pair of tennis shoes. He took the wadded napkin from his robe pocket and stuffed it down the front of his jeans, then made sure his t-shirt covered it completely, showing no bulge. He ran a comb quickly through his hair and then headed back downstairs. He took note of the time on the grandfather clock at the top of the staircase. Ten-thirty. The Gilliams would be here at noon, and he was very excited. How to pass the time until their arrival?

With that thought, he returned to his room and put a plaid flannel shirt over his t-shirt. He buttoned it from the neck down, then he knelt next to his bed and fished around beneath it, finally pulling a shoebox out. Lucien opened the box and shuffled through the contents, and when he found what he was looking for, his face lit up with delight. He put the item in the right hip pocket of his jeans and replaced the box, then he ran downstairs.

Mother was in the family room listening to music and flipping through a magazine that was likely older than he. "Mama, I am going outside to the courtyard to play. I just wanted you to know where I was," he told Rasia.

She looked up from her reading and smiled. "Okay,"

she began, a bit of trepidation in her voice. "Be good, Lucien, okay? I wouldn't want to have things end for you before they even begin."

"Yes, Mother, of course." He turned and walked through the foyer and out the front door of the house.

At the far end of the courtyard, there was a grouping of trees. Before Lucien had come under the control and watchful eyes of his 'nurses,' he had gone there alone to play quite often. It was his refuge and sanctuary. It was where he could be himself completely and do the things he wanted without observation.

When he arrived there, he looked around in surprise. The area he played in most often had grown over quite a bit, and he immediately began to clear sticks and leaves off of the area. Once it was clear, his eyes roamed over the ground anxiously until he saw what he was looking for, buried almost entirely under some leaves right at the edge of his area.

He cleared the leaves and knelt down. Before him on the ground was a metal box trap. He had gotten it years ago from the gardener's shed. The man had told him it was for catching critters that ate the vegetation on the property, but they didn't use it anymore, so Lucien had taken it for himself. Now he brushed the inside of the trap out with his hand and set it up. It was a bit of a struggle, as it had gained a bit of rust, but he got the job done.

Next, he took the napkin from down his pants and took out the chunk of now cold French toast, which he placed inside the trap. He then covered the top and sides of the contraption with leaves and sticks, then stood to observe his work. Perfect.

He wandered out of the wooded area and started to walk around the courtyard. While not much had changed out here, everything still seemed different, smaller almost. He knew this was because he was bigger; he had grown. He found a stick long enough to act like a walking stick, and as he strolled, he pushed around leaves and flowers or whatever else caught his attention. When he got to his old playset, he looked at it with disgust. What a baby he had been.

When Lucien had made a full circle around the courtyard and was satisfied that he had seen enough, he made his way back to the wooded area. While he didn't expect to have captured anything, he would check anyway, just in case. He was still about ten feet from the pile of leaves which hid the trap when he heard it. An animal had indeed been captured, and it was struggling a bit in the metal box, trying to find a way out.

Lucien moved the leaves off the top of the box and picked it up by the thin handle on top. He looked through the cage door to see a brownish-gray colored rabbit inside. It was still a baby, he thought. Probably less than a year old. He sat on the ground and carefully opened the door, putting his hand inside at the same time. He grabbed the bunny by the scruff of its neck firmly and pulled it out of the box, allowing the box to fall to the ground.

He looked around him cautiously, as though someone might be watching. As he did, he dug his free hand into the hip pocket of his jeans and pulled out his penknife, the one he had for years, and he had kept it hidden from everyone. It was his prized possession.

For the three years that Lucien had been forced to be in the presence of the nurses, he had satisfied his lust for blood with house mice. He had set up traps in the privacy of his room, but the result was an abundance of mice which ended up moving in, so to speak, and once they were discovered, his mother had the entire estate fumigated. This would be his first in a very, very long time, and the thought made him warm all over.

Lucien held the bunny up by its scruff until its face was directly across from his. "Hi, furry little bunny. You look afraid. Are you afraid?" The bunny had frozen in his hand in panic. "Yes, you are afraid, and you should be."

With a quick upward thrust, he buried the knife in the bunny's belly. It let out a squeal, and he twisted the knife and buried it deeper. The rabbit's blood was dripping out of its body and running down his hand onto the sleeve of his plaid flannel shirt. Some drops landed on his jeans, but the warm feel of the blood had Lucien in such ecstasy that he didn't even notice much less care.

When he was sure the bunny was dead, he laid it down on the ground before him. He had already determined what he would do: he wanted to see its insides, and he wanted to keep its skin for himself. It was so soft.

First, he cut the rabbit from under its chin down the

entire length of its belly. It was difficult to keep ahold of, as the blood had soaked its fur. He put his knife down and ripped its flesh open to get a good look inside. With his fingers, he poked at its organs. He knew what each was. He had no interest in learning here, this was strictly for self-satisfaction.

After about fifteen minutes of reveling in the death of the animal before him, he busied himself with skinning it, then he threw its bald carcass as far into the woods as he could. Wow, this was the best day ever! Not only was he free, but he had also been able to play the way he wanted without any trouble at all.

He wrapped the bloody hide in the cloth napkin and stuffed it down his pants. It was time to get back to the house.

He would have to clean up before Isabella, and her parents came. He would take the service entrance; no one would be using it because it was the weekend, and that way Mother wouldn't see him. Before she knew it, he would be spotlessly clean.

He marched toward the house with a smile of satisfaction on his face.

R.W.K. Clark

CHAPTER 8

"Happy birthday, Lucien!" Patrick, Rose, Isabella, and Mother were gathered around Lucien at the head of the long dining room table, a cake lit with ten bright candles before him. They had sung to him with gusto, and he knew that much of their happiness was based on the adult's belief that the boy had 'changed.'

When he returned from the courtyard, he had hidden his bloody clothes and showered, then made sure to don his very best outfit for Mother: black trousers, a crisp white button-down shirt, a black leather belt, and shiny leather dress shoes. When she saw him, her whole face lit up; she had been very pleased. She was easier for Lucien to manipulate now than ever before. Perhaps the suffering he had endured for the last three years had been just what was needed to gain control over the situation with his mother.

His guests were all looking at him and smiling happily, all except for his mother Rasia, that is. Lucien had noticed while they were singing that she wasn't participating. She had a fake smile on her face, and she seemed to be... sniffing at him while she stood next to him. When the song was over, and he went to blow out the candles, she had moved away from him, sitting about four seats down.

It was this particular behavior from Rasia that Lucien found most distasteful. She had done it more and more as he got older, and whether or not she thought he was aware of it was irrelevant; he was. He hated her, and he constantly felt unsafe around her, though he did not understand it.

There was a massive load of presents just waiting for him to tear them open, and he did so eagerly. Nothing impressed him, though. He was above childish toys, but he put on a smile and acted as enthusiastically as necessary to appease the grown-ups. The best gift he received was a card, hand-made by Isabella, with a mushy poem written inside in her own pen. That he would keep forever. The other things he would eventually tear to bits for fun.

By the time the group was done with the cake and ice cream, Lucien was losing his patience with the entire affair. He had been a prisoner in his own home for the last three years. He wanted to go hang out with his friend, maybe play some video games. Didn't they get that? But rather than complain, he continued his front until the two kids were given the okay to go about their own interests.

Lucien and Isabella took to the family room and shut the door firmly behind them. While she untangled the cords to the video game controllers, Lucien watched her. He wanted to tell her about the rabbit. She would understand.

"Guess what I did today, Isabella," Lucien began.

Without looking up, she answered him. "What? It could be just about anything. I would have gone nuts if I was finally free."

He remembered the warmth of the bunny's blood, then continued. "I visited my old spot in the woods, the one at the end of the courtyard."

Isabella looked up, her brow a bit creased. "What did you do there?" she asked with a light tone.

"Well, I cleared the leaves and crap from the ground, then I found my old box trap," he said.

She put the controllers down on the carpet and sat down next to him, leaning her back against the sofa. "So tell me."

Lucien began to fiddle with a button on his shirt nervously, but he was far from nervous. He recalled the wonderful experience in his mind so he could give his good friend all the details. He had to let it out to someone.

"I snuck a bite of my breakfast out with me, some French toast," he began. "When I found the box, I cleaned it up a little. It was tough and rusty, but I got it to set right."

"Did you catch anything, or do you not know yet?" Isabella asked softly.

He nodded. "I caught something almost right away. A bunny rabbit."

He was quiet for a moment, then he continued. "I took my knife with me when I went out too."

He looked up from his buttons then. Her face was

calm, but her eyes appeared a bit anxious, and Lucien wasn't sure why. He proceeded to fill her in on all the graphic details, and he told her how he had the rabbit's hide upstairs in his room. As he told the story, Isabella's breathing became more and more rapid, and then Lucien figured it out: she was enjoying this.

When he was finished, Isabella let out a long sigh. She closed her eyes and lay her head against the sofa. "I wish I had been there with you."

"Isabella, have you ever done them? You know, the things I like to do," he asked her.

She got a thoughtful look on her face for a moment, then said, "No, but I want to. I want to be with you next time."

"Why would you want to be with me?" Lucien asked.

Isabella simply shrugged. "Because it's a part of you, and you are a part of me."

Lucien reached over and took Isabella by the hand, and they sat quietly like that for some time. Yes, he thought to himself. This is the girl I will marry someday.

CHAPTER 9

The house was dead silent.

Rasia was resting on a bed in the spare room that she had made up for her own lustful purposes. As Lucien's tenth birthday had approached, she had decided that it would be best to have a room far away from his own in which to carry out her bloody escapades once the nurses were all gone. She had minor construction done, and soundproofing added, and what appeared to be a stylish, comfortable bedroom was now a chamber for sex and murder.

It was the only way she could satisfy her appetites, and they seemed to only be going stronger with each passing day.

In the last six months alone, she had killed a total of two hundred and forty men. Because each and every one of them had attempted to spill their disgusting seed inside of her, and she would have no part of it. The thought alone made her feel like she was covered in dirt and filth. No one would ever do that to her again, not after Cyril.

As she lay on the bed waiting for Martin Lamb to bring her next victim, she let her mind wander to Cyril and the all-too-brief love they had experienced together. Yes, she had indeed taken his life, but the emotion she had begun to feel for him had grown substantially. As she pondered his death, she often wondered what motivated her to do such an act to the ruler of the world and her first lover. She had no idea, but she suspected that the joining of their bodies and the bite which he gave her which she had so longed for had turned her into something no one suspected: a monster.

Now she missed him with a passion that burned and kept her awake at night, and not only for selfish reasons. She imagined that Lucien would be so very different had he the guidance of his father, not to mention she would not be raising him alone, blind to the facts of his nature. She often thought about drinking the boy's blood until his body was completely drained and he went limp in her arms, but she feared the Powers far too much to ever cross that line.

But she could smell his blood all the time, and it smelled more wonderful than a gourmet meal! She kept away from him as often as possible. She knew he likely wondered why she had erected a wall, but she didn't think he had figured it out. She knew that Lucien simply thought she hated him, and that was a price she was willing to pay to save her own wretched life.

She heard the light rapping of Martin at her door. She no longer bid him to enter, as he could not hear her anyway. Now he would simply knock, wait a moment, and then lead whatever random man into the room that he had chosen for her.

She was less than impressed with his latest choice. The man who came in had mousy brown hair and a substandard body, not to mention the fact that he dressed like a hobo. It would be easy to take his life, and she would revel in slurping down his already-infected blood.

Oh, how she missed the days when full-blooded humans roamed the Earth, but alas, they were all gone now. Oh, well, she thought, at least I have the stragglers of the Family to feed off of. The weaklings.

Martin left them, locking the door to the room behind him as he left, and Rasia sat up, naked, on the very edge of the bed. She looked the man over, then said to him, "What are you waiting for? You don't need clothing for what we are about to do."

Quickly he removed the rags he wore and made his way to her. She stopped him in his tracks.

"On your knees before me! I am your Queen!" Her voice was filled with anger at his lack of respect.

The man dropped to his knees in front of her on the bed, and she took his head by its hair roughly, burying his face between her legs. As he went to work on her, licking and sucking her violently, she thought, they are all only really good for one thing.

She lay back on the bed and spread her legs wide to give him better access, and he plunged his fingers deep inside of her. She bucked against him over and over, but would not even let him up for air. Finally, she was ready to feel him inside of her. She pulled him on the bed, and that was when she saw that his penis was limp. She looked at the carpet; he had ejaculated on the floor while he serviced her.

This infuriated Rasia. "How dare you! You are here for my good pleasure, not your own! You mangled piece of crap!" She grabbed him by the hair and jerked his head back hard. Then she grabbed his neck with her free hand and violently ripped his throat out, then buried her face in the ragged, gaping wound.

Rasia remained like that until he was drained, then she licked the blood from his neck and face. It was not the best tasting she ever had, and he left her still feeling... hungry.

Disgusted, she rose and went into the bathroom, where she showered and dressed. She then left the room to go to her own bed, making sure to lock the door behind her. Martin knew what to do; the room would look like brand new in the morning. She made a mental note to let Martin know how extremely displeased she was with his latest provision.

As she approached her bedroom door, she looked through the darkness to Lucien's room at the end of the hall. The boy stood in his door, which was open about eight inches. He was looking straight at her, smiling a toothy grin.

She did not smile back, she simply looked at him. He continued to smile as he gently shut his door. Rasia quickly locked herself in her room and leaned her back against the door for good measure. He knew, perhaps not specifically, but he knew.

Soon enough her boy would figure out the truth

about the world and who he really was, and Rasia dreaded the day.

∞

"Mom, I want to start spending more time with Lucien during the day." Isabella was seated at the island in the kitchen of the family home, her feet high off the ground and swinging playfully. She had been looking for the perfect opportunity to broach the subject, and that would be now when she was alone with her mother.

Rose turned to her daughter and studied her. "You know we are all cautious of Lucien, Isabella."

The girl grumbled a bit under her breath. "Lucien would never, ever hurt me, mother. You know that."

"What makes you think he wouldn't?"

Isabella shrugged. "Because we will marry one day, and he knows it. He is my friend, and he loves me."

Rose crossed her arms over her chest and continued to look at her beautiful daughter. Yes, she knew a marriage between the two children was inevitable, but the thought brought her great anxiety. Lucien was off, and the entire world that knew him was also aware of the fact, including his own mother.

"What do you have in mind?" Rose finally asked.

"Well," Isabella began, "Neither of us study anywhere but at home, and we are both done for the day by after lunch. Why can I not have two or three days a week to go play?"

Rose turned back to her sink full of dishes. "I think that is a bit much to start, child."

"Okay, mom, how about one day a week. Then if

you and dad relax a bit, maybe more later on?"

Rose smiled while her back was turned. Oh, the girl was smart! Bargaining, at such a young age, and the fact of the matter was that both her request and argument were reasonable and intelligent.

She turned back to Isabella, drying her hands on a dish towel. "I'll tell you what. I will talk to your father tonight and see what he says. If he is okay with trying it out, and if Rasia agrees, we will allow it. Fair?"

"Yes! Thank you, mommy!" Isabella ran to her and gave her a fierce hug, then she looked up into her mother's face. "You'll see. It will be okay."

Rose watched as her daughter ran off in excitement, and then the smile faded quickly from her face. Rasia had kept nothing from her and Patrick regarding Lucien. Probably she just needed moral support and advice, but also because she did not want to see Isabella hurt. Rasia preferred the girl to Lucien, and that was obvious.

But Rose knew all that the boy was capable of. She had no idea that Isabella was fully aware of all of Lucien's violent escapades and tastes. She thought her daughter to be fully innocent of the details, and as far as she was concerned, it should stay that way. What if he poisoned her mind and her thinking? What if he smelled the human in her and tried to have her blood for himself?

The thought scared Rose Gilliam to death.

But she had promised, and so tonight she would approach Patrick with their daughter's request. Deep inside she knew he would oblige, for he too believed the children to be betrothed to each other by the Powers themselves, or whoever it was that really ran the show down here on Earth. Rose hoped he would not allow it, but she knew he would.

She drew a ragged breath and turned back to her dishes, praying to the gods under her breath for guidance and mercy.

∞

"Lucien, my mother, is going to talk to my father tonight about me visiting alone more often," Isabella said into the telephone receiver. "I asked her, and it may only be one day a week at first, but I know they are going to let me!"

Lucien was silent at first on the other end. "Really?" he finally said. "Are you sure?"

"I'm sure!" Isabella had been so excited when she left the kitchen she had made a beeline for the phone. She couldn't wait to tell him.

Lucien said, "Well, then it is more important now than ever that we both mind our behavior and manners." He stopped to think. "I can't wait. I have wanted to share some of my most private secrets with you for so long!"

Isabella heard footsteps. "I have to go. I'll call you later." She hung up the phone gently, then turned and sat properly on the end of the loveseat. Her mother walked into the room.

"You should get yourself ready for your bath, Isabella. You will need to be turning in for the night soon enough." Rose took her daughter by the hand and, laughing, lifted the girl right up into the air effortlessly.

Isabella broke into hysterical laughter, then yawned. "I love you, Mommy."

"I love you too, Isabella," Rose replied. "I think you should wait to tell Lucien until I talk to Daddy. That way he doesn't get his hopes up, okay?"

Isabella nodded and smiled. "Okay."

It didn't matter to her that she had already disobeyed and then lied about it. It was meant to be. Soon enough she would become a part of Lucien's personal world fully and completely.

Isabella Gilliam could hardly wait.

∞

Lucien hung up the telephone and stared into space. When Isabella first visits, what should we do? He wanted to impress her beyond her imagination, so second best simply would not do.

First, he thought about setting his box trap and seeing what he could catch. No, he concluded. Too basic. If Isabella really wanted to get to know him, her first time would have to involve something far better than a rabbit or a squirrel.

He climbed the stairs to get ready for bed. He took a shower, constantly thinking about the situation. While he brushed his teeth, he still turned it over in his mind. When he finally climbed into his bed, he was almost obsessed with the predicament.

What could he do?

He turned off the lamp on his nightstand and stared

through the darkness at the ceiling. Nothing but the very best would do, for Isabella should only get to know the real him, and no bunny rabbit was going to demonstrate his reality. He began to finally doze off.

Suddenly, in the cloudy beginnings of his dreams, it came to him. Lucien's eyes flew open, and he sat straight up in his bed in the darkness. Out of nowhere, he had the solution, and it came to him with surprising violence.

He would get their first one from the park where he and Isabella had first met. He would offer her a human. Nothing could be better for their first time together.

It would be easy; he knew just what he would do and how he would lure them. He would go tomorrow, after his studies. He knew with surety Mother would let him; she would consider it a test.

Lucien lay back down on his pillow, a broad smile on his face. He was more excited than he could ever remember. He would mind himself perfectly tomorrow, even going out of his way to please Mother. It was the only way.

Finally, Lucien, future Master of the World, fell into a deep, contented sleep.

R.W.K. Clark

CHAPTER 10

Rasia walked into the classroom where she taught her son his lessons. It was bright and early; he would not arrive for another hour. She wanted their day to go well. He had behaved so wonderfully lately that she wanted to treat him with a bit of kindness in an effort to keep the behavior going.

As soon as she opened the door to the room, she sucked her breath in. Lucien was seated at his desk, working away. He turned to her and smiled brightly. Rasia was at a loss.

"Hi, Mama. I hope your morning has been good."

After overcoming her initial surprise, Rasia began to advance toward her desk, keeping her eyes on her son the whole time. "Yes, Lucien, it has been. You are here early, yes?"

He nodded at her, still smiling. "I wanted to get a head start on my science questions today."

"Good. You go ahead and work on that, and I will get organized for the day," she told him. She took a seat at her desk. "Lucien, I am more impressed with you every day. I hope you forgive me for the measures I took to straighten you out."

"Of course, Mother," he smiled as he lied through his teeth. "I don't even think about the nurses anymore."

Lucien went back to his assignments while Rasia busied herself sorting out the day's new ones. She was a bit stunned by Lucien, she had to admit. The difference in him now compared to three years ago was like day and night, and ever the cynic, Rasia was a bit suspicious. She was suspicious of everyone, though. Maybe she was not giving her son enough credit.

She pushed the thoughts out of her mind, and the two got about their day. Not only did he complete his science assignment with excellence, but he also attacked the new tasks she gave him with an eagerness that was completely uncharacteristic of him. He participated in discussing all the subject matter she presented, and he even asked highly intelligent questions that challenged her as well. By the time lunch arrived and they wrapped the day up, Rasia felt the first slight tugging of affection for the child that she had felt since his birth.

"Ah, Lucien. Wonderful day. You can go ahead and put your things away and go to lunch if you wish," she told him, putting her own papers and books together.

He put his books and papers neatly away in his desk and rose to leave the room. He had just opened the door to leave when Rasia stopped him.

"Oh, Lucien," she began. "I almost forgot. Rose called last night, and we spoke extensively. You have been doing very well, and we have decided that it might be a good idea for you to begin having Isabella over to visit now and again on a more regular basis. What do you think? Is this something you are ready to handle responsibly? I would hate for the girl to get… hurt."

Lucien struggled to control his excitement. He straightened his face before turning to his mother. "That would be wonderful. When do you think she will be able to come?"

Rasia busied herself with her papers. "We have planned to have her over on Wednesdays, and if things go well, she will visit more often. Maybe a few times a week, but on Wednesdays only in the beginning."

"Thank you," Lucien said. "I look forward to it."

He smiled at his mother and left the room, closing the door behind him. Foolish, they all were, but not concerning his Isabella. Her presence in his life, no matter how scarce, was all he wanted and needed.

He quickly ate lunch then went to his room to formulate a solid plan for Isabella's 'breaking in.' He sat at the desk in his room writing furiously in his notebook, and as he progressed, the evil grin on his little face grew. He was becoming more and more excited with each passing minute.

Tomorrow, Tuesday, he would ask Mother if he could walk to the park. There he would find someone, anyone, to bring home. How would he get them? That was the best part! Lucien had a vial of tranquilizer and a package of syringes which he had stolen from his mother's room just this morning, the same tranquilizer they had used on him on occasion when he was in the care of those apes Mother liked to call nurses. He would load up one of the syringes, and when he found a suitable victim, he would lure them here, to the woods at the end of the courtyard, and there he would drug them, tie them up, and together he and Isabella would have all the fun they wanted.

When he was finished outlining his plan, he took one of his backpacks and filled it with a roll of duct tape and some rope he had used in the past to tie up animals with. He also packed his pen knife, but along with that, he included a hunting knife he had stolen from the apron of one of the male kitchen workers a long time back. He had everything he needed to show his girl Isabella a very good time indeed.

He slung the backpack over his shoulder and headed downstairs. Mother was sitting in the dining room eating her lunch and enjoying a glass of wine.

"Mother, I am going outside to the courtyard. Is that alright with you?" He kept a pleasant smile and tone; he was Mother's good boy now, after all.

Rasia looked up. She had smelled him coming before seeing his face. "Of course. Enjoy the day; it is beautiful outside."

He nodded and turned, walking down the hall to the back entrance. He would put the pack safely under the shrubs in the wooded area. There it would wait for him and Isabella until it was time for fun and games on Wednesday.

He was more excited than he could remember being in a very long time indeed.

Lucien's study period seemed to drag on and on Tuesday morning. He tried hard to concentrate fully on his assignments, but his mind kept wandering to his walk to the park. He had made his request to go to his mother at the breakfast table that morning.

"I wondered if I could visit the park today Mother," Lucien had begun.

Rasia had looked up at him while taking a drink of her coffee. She said nothing right away, and this had made him just a little bit nervous. Would she refuse his request? She was definitely digesting it.

Lucien remained quiet and let her think. It was best not to nag her or try to talk her into it with slick words; she was someone who would see right through that behavior. No, he would let her take her time.

Finally, she cleared her throat. "I don't know, Lucien. Do you think you're ready for such a step? It has been a while since you have been out in the 'real' world." She kept her eyes on him, watching for how he would act.

But to Rasia's surprise, he remained very calm and controlled. "I know it has been, and to be honest, I am a bit nervous," he lied. "I just thought seeing something new would be good. If you don't think I'm ready…"

"No, no!" Rasia was choosing her words carefully. "I just want to know that you are going to be okay. That you won't perhaps fall backward a bit in the wrong direction."

She got quiet once again, Lucien remained collected.

She would let him go. She was acting as if she didn't want to offend him. It was a good sign.

Finally, Rasia spoke. "I'll tell you what, let's have our lessons, and if you are still in the mood to go to the park afterward, I will let you take an hour to visit there."

"Thank you, Mother," Lucien said carefully.

She continued. "If all goes well you can visit more often, okay?"

Lucien nodded. Awesome! He would go and find someone to lure away, and if for any reason he couldn't find someone, he would be paving the way to go and keep looking. His plan was working out beautifully.

Now he sat and pounded away at his work, his mind wandering, and his eyes glancing at the clock every thirty seconds or so. If there was anything he had learned during the three years he spent under the care of his 'nurses,' it was patience. The time would eventually come, and until then he would contain himself appropriately.

At eleven-thirty Rasia excused him, telling him she had a meeting, and that she wanted him to take his lunch before he ventured out. She would not return home until late afternoon or early evening, so if he needed anything, he was to go to Martin Lamb. Lucien thought about giving his mother a hug goodbye for good measure but knew that the behavior would be way too unusual, and would likely spread suspicion in her mind. He opted to simply keep up his polite façade, but he was more than glad that Rasia would be gone for most of the day.

"I hope your meeting goes well, Mother," he said. "And thank you again for letting me go to the park. I will see you when you get home."

"Yes, and if you are in bed, I will look in at you," she replied. "Take advantage of this opportunity today to earn a little bit more trust, Lucien."

As he walked out of the room, Rasia got a good smell of his blood. It made her skin crawl and awakened her thirst. Maybe she would take some time to ride around and 'hunt' for herself a bit. The men Martin had been bringing her had been sadly lacking lately. It would be the perfect opportunity.

Lucien left the classroom with a smile on his face. Not only was he being allowed to go to the park without supervision, but he would also have most of the house to himself when he returned. He didn't intend to keep the person in the house; no, they would be tightly bound and kept out in the clearing. He would check on them in the night a couple of times because it would be easy to slip in and out after bedtime. It was already in his mind that he would make sure the person was fully tranquilized until they met their fate. It wouldn't do to have them escaping and running to tell someone what had happened.

No, that would be his undoing, and he wouldn't have it.

His lunch consisted of a grilled ham and cheese sandwich and potato chips. Lucien had apple juice with his meal. He basically inhaled the food, eating it all in just a few quick bites. He knew that the servants would report to his mother how much he had eaten. Mother was big on Lucien getting the proper nutrients. He knew he would need his strength, so he ate it all.

When he was finished with his meal, he grabbed a light jacket from the hall closet near the courtyard exit and made his way out to the wooded area. There he prepared one syringe, which he put in the inside pocket of the jacket. He then took in a long breath, drawing the early afternoon air into his lungs. Then he looked in the direction of the park and began walking.

It would be a great day.

∞

Lucien sat on the park bench, his hands in his pockets and his foot kicking at the rocks on the ground. There was really no one visiting the park at all; a couple of adults had walked through, but they took no notice of his presence. A few children were playing, but they were all with adults, and he did not feel like dealing with that kind of hassle.

He had no interest in taking a female. Lately, more and more girls and women caught his eye among the servants. After all, those were the only people he came into contact with. He did know that there was something special about girls, something he seemed almost able to… smell. No, the first person to fall victim to his little scheme of presentation for Isabella would be male. Boy or man, it made no difference to him.

He was supposed to stay only an hour, but as his time drew to a close and he had no luck, he thought he would give it thirty minutes more. Pushing it was no big deal; Mother was gone, and if Martin even noticed, he would tell Mother he had been in his room and forgot to check in right away when he returned. No sweat.

After another fifteen minutes passed, Lucien was just about ready to give up. The children and their grown-ups had all left, and now he sat alone in the playground area. That was when he heard the voice behind him.

"Why are you here alone? Are you waiting on a playmate, or your mother or father?" Lucien turned to find a young man of about twenty standing on the walkway behind him. He had short light brown hair and kind brown eyes with long lashes. Lucien couldn't tell if he was really nice, or if he was leering at him. For clothing, the man wore jeans, a blue button-down shirt, and a pair of white tennis shoes.

Lucien's sick soul smiled wide inside of him. Perfect.

He pretended to be apprehensive about the man's presence. "No, I'm just hanging out. Really, I can't remember what direction to walk in to get back to my house."

"Oh," the man replied. "My name is Phillip. Maybe I can help you."

He slowly approached Lucien while he held his hands up in the air. He was trying to show the boy that he would be safe with him. "Where do you live?"

"I live in the big white house," Lucien said innocently.

The man's eyes widened. "You mean the White

House? Is your mother our Queen?"

"My mother is Rasia. Do you know her?" Now Lucien was beginning to realize how easy this was really going to be.

Phillip shook his head, but his eyes were alight with excitement. "No, not as of yet, I do not know her personally, but everyone knows who the Queen is. I could get you home safely. Do you think she would have time to meet me today?"

Lucien stood and offered his first smile. "I am sure. She will be pleased that you helped me to get home." He offered his hand to the stranger, looking as pitiful as he could.

Phillip took Lucien's hand in his. "No problem, Kiddo."

"Ok," Lucien said as they began walking in the direction of the house.

Phillip smiled back at him, and the two began the walk to take Lucien home. It was only about a fifteen or twenty-minute walk, and Lucien knew they would be there in no time, so he made an effort to engage the man in conversation the whole way. He talked about his studies, and how he hated certain subjects. Phillip related to him in a very friendly manner, and his comfort with Lucien made the boy more excited to subdue him than ever.

They were finally approaching the property when Lucien spoke up. "We do not use the main entrance in the front; I go in the back, by the courtyard." They began to walk around in the direction of the rear entrance. "Oh," Lucien continued. "I need to get my backpack from the woods. It's right over there." He pointed in the direction, and he and Phillip began to head that way.

Once they were at the clearing, Lucien began to act like he did not know where the bag was. He looked around, here and there, under bushes and behind trees. "Would you mind checking under that bush there, Phillip?"

The man bent down and looked. "I see it, Lucien. Here, I will get it for you." He was nearly on his face on the ground trying to retrieve the bag. That was when Lucien uncapped the syringe and buried it in Phillip's backside, right through his denim jeans. He pushed the plunger in fast.

Phillip jerked his head up, and all of a sudden his eyes glazed over. "What...?" was the only word that escaped from his mouth. He passed out cold on the dirt and leaves that covered the ground. Lucien smiled. So far, so good.

Now he got the bag out himself and proceeded to tie the man up using the strongest knots he had ever learned. He had done a lot of research on the Internet and practiced each and every one. For binding this man, he used the Palomar knot, and he was sure to keep the knot on the wrists out of reach of the man's fingers.

Next, he bound the man's feet, and duct taped him around the mouth and eyes with plenty of tape. Finally, Lucien dragged the man's limp body and hid it up against the trunk of a big tree, where all view of him was hidden by a broad-leafed bush. He then stood back to observe his work. The man was completely out of sight.

He gathered his bag and began to walk to the house, smiling. The tranquilizer would keep the man out from between four and six hours. It was now nearly two in the afternoon so he would give him another shot right around five-thirty, right after he ate his dinner.

It couldn't have gone more smoothly.

CHAPTER 11

Lucien was humming when he walked into the house, his backpack slung over his shoulder. He wanted to see what the weather was going to be like for the next day, then he planned to pack the bag with the 'toys' he and Isabella would need. Finally, he would call her and give her a couple of important directives.

He walked into the family room and found Martin Lamb seated before the television. He was watching some political program which was talking about how the world was in a much better place under the Queen's leadership.

"Do you know what the weather is going to be like tonight and tomorrow Martin?" Lucien began. "Isabella is going to visit tomorrow, and I am hoping we do not expect rain."

"Yes, I do," Lamb replied. "They said sunny and warm. Looks like you're all set, kiddo."

Lucien forced a smile and thanked him. He had Martin's 'kiddo,' alright. He made his way up to his room where he unpacked the remainder of the tape and rope, then he prepared another syringe full of the tranquilizer before putting all of his things safely out of sight. Next, he sat at his desk and dialed Isabella's number on the telephone.

"Hello," said Rose Gilliam when she answered.

Lucien cleared his throat and used his most innocent voice. "Hi, Mrs. Gilliam. It's Lucien. Is Isabella able to come to the phone?"

"Sure, Lucien, just a minute." The phone went silent, and a few seconds later Isabella came on the line.

"Hey, how are you today," Lucien began. He wanted to be sure Rose hung up the other extension.

Isabella giggled. "I'm good. I'm excited to visit tomorrow. Are you?"

"More than you know. Are you on the main phone, or in your room?"

Isabella answered. "Main."

"Is your mom by you?"

"No," the girl replied. "She's in the kitchen. We're safe."

Lucien breathed a sigh of relief. "Make sure you bring a pack. Fill it with toys or books or whatever, but at the bottom, you need to bring clothes to wear during our 'playtime.' Make sure they won't be missed by your mom, okay?"

"No problem. I know just the ones," she said. Lucien could hear the eagerness in her voice.

"Are you sure you want to do this, Isabella?" He would not force her; he wanted her to participate on her own free will.

"Yes," she said. "You know I do. I love you, Lucien."

He waved off the comment mentally. Neither of them knew what love was, but she was his best friend, and he couldn't be more appreciative to have someone to share his secrets with.

"I'll see you tomorrow after lunch then," he said. "I'm excited too, Isabella."

They said their goodbyes and Lucien hung up the phone softly. He then went into the bathroom and looked in the mirror. There were a couple pieces of wood and grass in his hair and on his jacket. He brushed his hair and took his jacket off. Then he went down to the family room with Martin Lamb. He wanted to pass the time until supper.

"Martin, do you want to play a game with me?"

The man turned to him, a look of sheer surprise on his face. "I'm afraid I'm not very adept at video games, Lucien," he said with a chuckle.

"Well, we could play cards, or dominoes, or something," he replied. "I just don't want to hang around here all bored, and I'm caught up on all my lessons."

Martin smiled, looking pleased. "Sure, kiddo." Lucien got the cards from the hall table, and the two sat cross-legged on the floor. "What do you want to play?" Martin asked.

"How about poker?" Lucien suggested.

"Ha! Now there's a game I have a chance of winning." The two laughed as Lucien shuffled, stacking the deck as he did.

Foolish man.

Supper consisted of Lucien's favorite: chili dogs and French fries with cheese sauce. Martin ate with him. Even though Lucien had beaten the man, winning a dollar-fifty in pennies from the penny jar, the man was pleased to be in his company.

They ate together telling jokes and laughing. Lucien knew that if he wanted to remain on his mother's good side, it was important to behave with everyone. The day would come when he would wipe the woman off the face of the Earth if he had his way, but for now, he had to play the game. He had figured that out well.

After supper, Lucien let Martin know that he was going out to the courtyard for some fresh air. He had a book in his hand and the syringe in his jacket. At first, it looked like Martin might suggest joining him, but when he saw the book, he got the hint: the boy wanted some alone time.

So, he left the house humming the same tune he had hummed when he came home from the park. He crossed the courtyard glancing behind him all the way. No Martin following him or watching him. Good.

He entered the wooded area and immediately heard Phillip's moaning. It was weak, and there was no movement from the bushes, but the man was indeed awake. Lucien's timing had turned out to be perfect.

He moved the branches of the bushes aside until he could see the man. He was no longer on his back; now he was on his side, and his clothes were covered in dirt. He had obviously been rolling around out here for a bit.

This meant that Lucien would have to come out a few times in the night. He sighed. Oh well, better safe than sorry.

He remained silent as he removed the syringe from his jacket and uncapped it. He then stood and watched as Phillip began to moan and squirm with more strength. He was coming around better now, but Lucien could not help but take a moment to revel in the sight of him struggling. It brought happiness to his soul.

After watching him for a bit, he finally walked toward him, kneeling down in the dirt beside him. He stared for only a minute longer, then he drove the needle into the man's thigh and pushed the plunger. Phillip immediately began to weaken once again.

"When you wake up next time, keep it quiet. I'm watching you, and if you don't, you will pay for it sooner rather than later," Lucien said. He recapped the needle and watched as the man fell back into a drugged haze.

Now he knelt back down and ran his fingers over the duct tape that covered Phillip's eyes and mouth. He traced the eyes and the lips with amusement, then stroked the skin on his face.

"Don't worry, Phillip," Lucien told him softly. "It will only last as long as we want it to."

He giggled at his own joke, then took his book and headed to the gazebo. It wouldn't do for Martin to look out the window and not see him reading his book. He had to keep up appearances.

After another twenty minutes in the courtyard,

Lucien went back to the house, still humming. The night was going to be falling, and the lights in the family room were already shining brightly out into the early evening. Lucien could see his mother standing with Martin Lamb. He was probably filling her in on Lucien's day.

Good, the boy thought. It had been an extraordinary one.

∞

Lucien visited Phillip at eleven, and the man had been just beginning to stir. He gave him another injection and left him. He didn't visit him again until nearly four. He knew he would have to prolong the period between shots, and he would have to sneak out before he and mother held classes in the morning. He took care of that at seven using the back entrance quietly. The man had still been sleeping, but he was still alive.

Classes went surprisingly fast for Lucien that Wednesday. Even though he was looking forward to a lot, he seemed to be able to focus quite well on his work and even enjoyed doing it. His mother laughed with him and cracked a couple of silly jokes, and this told him that Martin had given her a glowing report on his behavior. He was pleased.

After his lessons, he went down for lunch, and he ended up eating alone. Rasia had yet another meeting in town. This happened often, but he had never paid so much attention before, and he found himself resenting her. How did a woman like her come to lead people, anyway?

Yes, Lucien knew they were not normal 'people,' not the kind he read about in books anyway. No one on the planet was, but he was just starting to really pay attention to this fact. What really interested him lately was 'why.' With patience and determination, he would figure it all out.

But today, he had other plans.

He ate quickly and went to the family room. Isabella would be here within the hour. He would not give the man another shot. He would rather have him awake for the coming ordeal, or at least a little conscious.

Martin Lamb entered the room. "Lucien, I have an engagement in town myself. If you need anything, just have one of the servants tend to your need. Isabella should be here soon, so you should be fine."

"Yes, Martin," Lucien replied. "Have a good meeting. See you later."

The man smiled at him and nodded before leaving. Oh, things were getting better all the time.

He picked up a magazine from the table in front of him and began to read. He couldn't focus on the content, but it was best to not look too excited, at least in his opinion. After about fifteen minutes, he finally heard the bell from the back entrance, and it took all the strength he had in him to remain where he was and wait for the servant to bring his guest to him.

Isabella appeared at the door to the family room, a big smile on her face and her pack on her back. Rose and Patrick were both with her, and though they were smiling as well, their eyes betrayed their nervousness. Did they not want to leave Isabella because his mother and Martin were away? Did they even know?

"Hello, Lucien," Patrick began. "You are looking well. How is your day going?"

Lucien stood and tossed the magazine back onto the table. "I'm good, Mr. Gilliam. Glad to see Isabella!" With that, the girl walked all the way into the room and dropped her pack on the floor next to the desk.

She turned to her parents. "We'll be fine, guys." She was obviously aware of their apprehension.

Rose spoke. "Your mother told me she would be in conference today, and that Mr. Lamb is away as well. Do you need us to do anything before we leave?"

"No," Lucien replied. "We have the servants. We are just going to play. Probably video games and hang out in the courtyard, if that's okay with you."

Both the Gilliams nodded and their faces relaxed. Lucien wanted them to have no qualms about leaving Isabella there. The sooner they left, the better.

"If there are any problems at all, I will be sure either Isabella or I call you right away," he promised.

Rose smiled. "I appreciate that. Now, you two be good." She turned to Patrick. "Well, I guess we should get going then."

Isabella gave both of her parents an obligatory hug and kiss, and they finally turned to go. She and Lucien immediately headed to the video game console and turned it on. He looked at her knowingly; it would be better if they played with it for a half-hour or so, just until they knew they were in the clear.

The two kids began playing a racing game together, and they even lost track of time for a bit. Nearly an hour passed of uninterrupted play before Lucien said, 'Look, it's almost two. I think we're safe." He flipped the power off on the game, and they both sat still, listening. The house was quiet except for the normal sounds coming from the direction of the kitchen.

"What time are your parents planning to pick you back up?" he asked.

She smiled. "Not until seven. When will your mom be back?"

"Later tonight," he said. "Come up to my room. I need to grab my bag, then I will take you and introduce you to our new friend."

A curious look crossed her face. Of course, she couldn't know the details of what he had planned. He did not intend to force anything on her, but she wanted to watch, and he wasn't about to do this thing halfway. He just hoped she could stomach the ride.

They took the stairs two at a time, and once Lucien had retrieved his backpack, he dug around in it. He took a fresh needle and filled it with the tranquilizer before capping it and tucking it into the outer pocket of the bag.

"What's that for?" Isabella asked, her eyebrows raised in curiosity.

Lucien smiled. "This will keep our friend quiet if he starts to act up." He watched her face, trying to read her for any negative reaction, but she displayed none. She simply smiled and nodded.

"It wouldn't do to get caught," she said.

He nodded. "No, it wouldn't."

Also in the backpack were a straight razor, a paring knife from the kitchen, a couple of towels, and a cigarette package with two cigarettes in it. He also produced a disposable lighter. These weren't for smoking; they were for fun. Isabella didn't even ask him about them.

Lucien flung the pack onto his shoulder, and the two went back to the family room, where Isabella retrieved her own bag. "What should I do with this?"

"Okay, did you bring different clothes?" he asked.

She nodded in response.

"Take them up and change into them now. The ones you have on will have to be clean for you to wear home, and the others I will have to get rid of for you. Just change. I will wait for you right here."

Isabella flounced off toward the stairs once again, and Lucien paced back and forth waiting on his friend.

In only about ten minutes she returned, free of her bag. She was wearing a pair of mid-thigh cut-offs and a raggedy old playland t-shirt.

"When did you go to playland?" he asked her.

She smiled. "I didn't. It was a gift from my mother's sister. I do my chores in it sometimes."

Satisfied with her clothes, Lucien took her by the hand and together they made their way out to the courtyard.

As the two neared the woods, the sound of Phillip moaning and groaning grew. Isabella turned to Lucien. "Is it a man?"

Lucien simply nodded and continued to lead her to the large bush behind which Phillip was hidden. He moved the branches for her so she could reach the man, then followed her lead. Phillip was lying on his back once again. He was wet with sweat, and his face and hair were matted with dirt.

"Who is he?" Isabella asked softly as she stared at the sight of the bound man with wonder.

"Just someone I came across at the park," Lucien replied.

The two watched as he began to struggle even more at the sound of their voices. Finally, Lucien broke his reverie and placed his bag on the ground. He opened it and began to take all the items out one at a time, lining them up neatly on the ground.

"Isabella, you do not have to do anything if you don't want," he told her. "If you want to just watch, I'm okay with that, but you promise you will never tell anyone about me?"

She nodded vigorously. "Of course. It is our secret, Lucien."

She backed up a bit and took a seat on a large flat rock next to the tree trunk. Her eyes were wide with wonder. She knew that what she was about to see could never be unseen, and something inside of her cringed at that fact. But there was also something else inside of her that was hungry for what was about to happen, and that thing was much stronger than the first.

The children could smell the fear and confusion that were emanating off of the man's sweaty, filthy body. It gave them both goosebumps of excitement. Deep inside Isabella could hardly wait.

Lucien sat cross-legged in the dirt next to the man's squirming body. He held the straight razor firmly in his hand, and he looked at the gleaming steel of the blade. After a short moment, he began to cut the denim jeans off of Phillip, cutting the legs length-wise from top to bottom, until they simply fell to the ground around his legs.

Lucien had cut the flesh on his legs in a couple of spots, and this had spurred the man to put up a much stronger fight, so the boy took the syringe and administered a fraction of the drug into his leg, just enough to settle him down without knocking him out. Phillip relaxed quite a bit, but his moaning continued. Lucien looked at Isabella. Her eyes were glassed over, and she was smiling.

Phillip was wearing white brief underwear. If he were alone, Lucien would have removed them, but he did not want Isabella to see this man naked. He would leave them on him. He turned his attention to the blue button-down shirt. He simply laid down the razor and took the shirt in his hands, ripping it open. It gave easily.

Phillip's hands were bound in the front, so Lucien was forced to use the razor to remove the shirt completely, but it took only a few seconds. Now Phillip's breathing was a bit labored; he was panicked and confused all at the same time. This pleased Lucien to no end.

"Do you know what is happening to you, Phillip?" he asked the sweaty, dirty man.

Phillip shook his head furiously.

"Do you remember me?" Lucien asked.

Phillip nodded very slowly.

"The biggest mistake of your life was to offer to escort me home," he told Phillip. "For the next hour or so, you will find yourself regretting that decision more than ever."

The man began to shake violently as he lay there. Lucien watched him, smiling eagerly. He glanced at Isabella, half expecting to see her turning a little green around the gills, but she was holding her own. She did not even notice him looking at her; she was too busy watching this man, who was clothed in nothing but fear and underwear.

Next, Lucien took the straight razor and ran its blade across the man's forehead, cutting a deep straight line. Phillip began to scream against the duct tape, but it was too muffled to draw any attention. The two children laughed out loud as the blood oozed from the wound.

The blood began to flow freely, and that was when both Lucien and Isabella took notice of its scent. It was strong and sweet, like a dessert that beckoned as it baked. Its aroma was so delicious-smelling that it was almost unbearable.

To Lucien, this was very interesting. He had hurt only animals during his 'playtimes' before. When he had stabbed the nanny, he had not been in the presence of the body long enough to notice this scent, and none of the animals' blood smelled so sweet. He looked at Isabella, and she looked to be in a trance. A bit of spittle was pooling up on her bottom lip. Her mouth was watering, as was Lucien's.

Now he took the razor and ran the blade deep into the flesh of Phillip's upper right arm. Blood spurted out, then dripped grotesquely to the ground. Lucien did the same to his left arm. Both of the children were hypnotized by the sight and smell of the man's freshly spilled blood.

"Do you smell that?" Lucien asked Isabella.

She nodded. "It is the best thing I have ever smelled before. Who knew that people smelled like that inside?"

Phillip sounded like he was crying now, but the tears were not escaping the seal of the duct tape. The two kids watched him as his chest heaved with his sobs, and they were both entertained by his grief and panic. Both of them found it to be invigorating.

Next came Phillip's legs. Lucien dragged the razor over the flesh of his thighs, over his knees, and down the firm bone of his calves, one at a time; when he was cutting Phillip's thighs he let the blade go deep into the flesh and muscles. The man tried to scream in pain but to no avail. Lucien was half done with the second leg when Phillip's body went limp; he had passed out cold.

Now the smell of the blood pouring from the body before them was almost unbearable to Lucien. Isabella didn't move, but she was licking her lips feverishly, and she seemed to be in a trance. To Lucien, the blood was calling to him, and it seemed to be doing so out loud. It was all he could do just to resist the urge to… taste it.

Finally, he took the blade firmly in his hand and plunged it into Phillip's stomach, right under his rib cage, in the very center. With one fluid motion, he cut a straight line all the way down to the man's groin. Then he cut across, from left to right. He wanted to see what Phillip looked like inside.

The smell of the blood was suddenly more than Lucien could bear. He was no longer aware of Isabella, or even the ground or the trees. All he saw was the bloodied body of the man on the ground before him, and he knew he was going to taste the aromatic red fluid that was gushing from him. He took one look at Phillip's mangled mid-section and knew that he would not indulge his temptation from that area. He looked that man over and then his eyes rested on the most appetizing part of the body, one that he had not yet violated.

Phillip's throat.

Lucien moved so that he was seated at the top of Phillip's head. He lifted the unconscious man's chin and drew the blade over his throat with a quick swipe. More blood shot out, and with that, Lucien put his lips and mouth over the source of the flow.

Phillip's blood filled Lucien's mouth rapidly, so fast

he had difficulty keeping up. He slurped at the blood, swallowing it and letting it fill him. He could suddenly hear the sound of his own heartbeat; it was deafening in his ears. The noise his own blood made as it coursed through his veins was suddenly audible as well, and his head was spinning pleasantly. This man's blood was like a drug!

He continued to drink, and when he realized that the flow had stopped, he began to lick at the wound until it was clean. Lucien sat up and stared into the blue sky. He had never felt so complete, so fulfilled, in his whole life.

Suddenly he remembered Isabella. His eyes snapped open, and he looked at her, expecting her to either be gone or to be vomiting. She surprised him, though. She sat, steadfast on her rock, looking at Lucien, a smile playing on her lips. There was no repulsion on her face whatsoever.

"What does it taste like?" Isabella asked Lucien softly.

He glanced down at the dead man on the ground and then looked back at the wide-eyed girl before him. "It's hard to say, exactly. Like my birthday, I think. Yes, he tastes like everything good."

The two sat in silence for a moment, then Lucien asked her, "Do you want to try?"

Isabella did not answer him right away; she looked to be thinking hard. Finally, she spoke. "I don't think I'm ready yet. Something tells me it's not my turn yet."

Lucien only nodded, then turned his attention back to Phillip. He would have to drag the body further into the woods. Animals would find it and eat it before anyone ever ventured out here. He just couldn't seem to take his mind from the magnificent flavor that still filled his mouth. Oh, he never knew how good it could be!

After about ten minutes of peace and quiet, Lucien finally spoke. "Would you help me drag him further in? Then we can head inside and get cleaned up before it's time to eat supper."

Isabella stood. "What's for supper, anyway? I'm starving!"

The two looked at each other and burst out laughing. Yes, Phillip had proved to be quite an appetizer indeed. Lucien and Isabella would consume their upcoming meals with great zeal indeed.

∞

Now Lucien and Isabella sat at the table in the dining room, hefty slices of pizza steaming on their plates before them. They had come in and got cleaned up and changed without even seeing another living soul. Sitting here together and enjoying the rich food and cold soda pop was like having a celebration meal.

"Isabella, are you okay?" Lucien asked, then took a bite of his pizza.

She finished chewing her own mouthful, then replied, "Of course. No worries, Lucien. I had a lot of fun. I can't wait 'til next time."

They continued eating, then she added, "I might even try it next time myself."

She didn't look at him, but she had said it clearly. Yes, Lucien knew then that no matter what the future held for either him or Isabella, she was the girl for him. There was no question in his mind.

They finished their meals and then went into the family room to enjoy their video games.

Once again they were two young children, enjoying their games and each other's company. When it was time for Isabella to leave, Lucien's heart sank, and he gave her a heartfelt hug as her parents stood watching.

He would plan a surprise for her. It wouldn't be at her next visit, but it would be better than ever. It would be just for her.

∞

Rasia entered the house and met complete quiet. There was not even the sound of the television echoing through the halls. That meant that Martin had retired after returning from his own engagements. She wondered about Lucien and found herself worried that he had murdered everyone in the entire house.

She found him sleeping peacefully, though and breathed a sigh of relief that was audible. It seemed that her troubled, somewhat defective son had finally come around, and it pleased her. Now, if he only kept it up.

She showered and climbed into her own bed. There was no time for playing tonight, for her day had worn her out. One of the young politicians who was to be learning the New Way was to be initiated today as one of her personal servants. She had hand-picked him for the spot. She intended him to begin mentoring Lucien, but he had not shown up for his initiation ceremony. His name was Phillip Morgan, and she had her people searching for him even now.

It was not like any member of the family to duck out on plans made by the Queen. To do so meant certain punishment, and it was honestly not even their nature. They were driven to obey by the spirit living inside of them. That was why she was so disturbed by the no-show.

As she drifted off to sleep, she thought, oh well, they will track him down. It was certainly just a misunderstanding…

Then Rasia DeSai fell fast asleep.

R.W.K. Clark

CHAPTER 12

"Happy birthday, Isabella," Lucien said softly to the blossoming young girl seated next to him. He gazed at her as he spoke the words, and even reached out and stroked her long blond hair. She turned to him and smiled, her blue eyes shy.

"Thank you, Lucien."

The two were seated on a comfortable oak yard swing at the Gilliams. The stars were shining in the deep evening sky, and the moon was shining on them in full. A light breeze blew through the air, tousling her long curls, and she looked beautiful to Lucien.

At thirteen, Isabella was indeed growing into a striking young woman. She was tall and slender, with high budding breasts and a tiny waist. One knew that she would one day be drop-dead gorgeous, and no one knew this as well as Lucien. He supposed he loved her, at least, as much as he had ever 'loved' someone.

Tonight he would tell her the secret he had kept inside since his own thirteenth birthday, the one that explained everything to him about what he was. He waited for her own thirteenth because he wanted her to have a wonderful day. He didn't want her spoiled by the news, even if he had told her months before. He was sure it would have a negative effect, somehow, on their relationship.

∞

On the evening of his own thirteenth birthday, just four months before, Lucien and his mother Rasia had a celebration dinner alone, just the two of them. It was not often Rasia did this with her son, but when she did, she took it seriously.

The dinner was exceptional, her words soft and kind. She praised him for becoming such a studious, intelligent, and self-controlled young man. They talked about how trustworthy he had become, and she even stated how she looked forward to beginning to groom him as he stepped into his rightful position and heritage.

Suddenly, Lucien had understood that his mother had too much wine, and her tongue was a little looser than she would have liked. As she continued to talk on and on, it suddenly came out that he was a vampire, and not only that, he was born of a witch as well, his own mother Rasia. The information, though it knocked the wind out of him, did not completely surprise him. Yes, his mother had kept him sheltered and naïve to a point, but he was far from stupid.

But now she sat here and began to tell Lucien, in great detail, her own story, the tale of who she was, and by the time she related to him the night she killed his own father, Lucien was enraged.

"You are no ordinary young man. I do not mean because you will lead the world," Rasia had begun. "No, not just that. You are much more, as all of us are."

Lucien had been a bit confused at first. "Much more?"

Rasia had lifted her wine glass to her lips and drained it, then began to pour another. "Yes, Lucien. Your father, Cyril DeSai, my husband, was a vampire, and not just any vampire. He was the beginning of all, the father of the family."

"A… a… vampire?" Lucien felt a bit stunned emotionally, but mentally it all made immediate sense. "Like in books?"

Rasia nodded. "He was indeed a vampire, born in France centuries ago to a winemaker who came from a family of winemakers. He himself had made wines, even then. He had a beautiful wife and beloved children. He had been wealthy and held the respect of the entire town in which he resided.

"But his family, all of them, had fallen victim to an unseen murderer. The killer had not shown him the same mercy. No, instead he had bitten the young vintner and cursed him to an eternity of walking the Earth, lonely and craving blood. He had started to build a family of his own again on several occasions, but living humans had always discovered who he was, and he always ended up running. Running and hiding.

"He told me of his refuge in the side of the cliff on the ocean, where he would hide from the hunters until it was safe to begin again. The cycle had been started and ended countless times, and each time he had been left lonely, angry, and dreaming of a time when he would not only have a family but find his one true mate, his queen.

"No other before me had ever been considered. To him I was the perfect woman to be his eternal mate: we were the same, mind, body, and spirit. My evil darkness complimented his to a tee, and he wanted to possess me. He wanted to provide me with eternal life.

"There it was. Everything I needed to hear he had just revealed to me. Inside I was ecstatic. I had found him, the ever-elusive vampire of my ancestors' theories and dreams.

"He began the Family by changing Isabella's own father, Patrick Gilliam and three of his friends as they enjoyed a SCUBA diving trip in Honduras. They, in turn, began to change others, and now the world is ours."

"Don't you mean 'mine'?" Lucien asked her darkly.

Rasia laughed. "Yes, I suppose I do. But there is more."

"More?"

Now she simply nodded. "Yes. I was, am, a witch. You are the first of your kind, both vampire, and witch, and this is why you have struggled so," she told him with a smile on her face. "Don't be angry with me, Lucien. No one could know what you would be or what you would become. You were an experiment, so to speak."

"How could you keep me in the dark?" Lucien screamed, standing from the table and throwing his napkin at her. His eyes blazed, and Rasia saw in him his father, bold, dark, and dangerous. She realized then that she had approached the topic quite wrong, and the buzz she felt from the wine began to dissipate.

"Lucien, you need to understand that we did not know what you would be," Rasia was fumbling at her words, repeating things. "You were the first vampire and witch offspring ever to take a breath. You had to be watched until I was able to determine the truth about you."

Lucien listened, but he did not truly hear her. He was visualizing wrapping his hands around her skinny neck and ripping her head from her body, as she had said she had done to his father. Then he would drink her blood, just as a proper vampire would.

"Obviously it was for the best that I did this," she continued, "Look at how you had to live until you turned ten. You were out of control, and you were dangerous."

Little do you know, Lucien thought. Then he slowly walked around the long dining room table. Rasia kept her eyes locked on his; even now she didn't trust him.

When he reached the end of the table furthest from her, he charged at her with all his might. Rasia stood, feeling panic for only an instant. He was as fast as lightning, and she hardly had time to think. She closed her fist and swung her arm at her thirteen-year-old son and hit with great force. She lifted him off his feet and sent him flying backward. He crashed into the table, slid down the length of it, and hit the wall. His body had smashed through the paneling, and Lucien lay in a crumpled heap among the rubble.

"I know it was hard news, but you are thirteen, you are a man now," Rasia said, her voice as calm as if nothing had happened. "You will grow in stature, and yes, in power, until one day, when you may even be able to defeat me. But that day is not today."

Rasia turned on her heel and left the dining room, leaving her son crumpled on the floor, his pride injured and his mind racing. Yes, it explained it all, and to be honest, it made him feel even more secure in who and what he was. Yes, he would certainly someday end her life as if he were doing nothing more than blowing out a candle on one of his birthday cakes.

∞

Now, months later, he sat here on the swing with Isabella remembering that night, and he felt it his full responsibility to tell Isabella what he really was, and he was deeply concerned that it would spur her to reject him. How did he broach the subject with her? What could he say to make it alright? After all, he was a hybrid, not even human. He was a vampire, and he was a witch.

"Isabella, I need to tell you something," Lucien began. "It's something my mother told me on my past birthday, something I think you should know."

The girl looked at him, calmly and expectantly, a slight smile on her lips. "Yes, Lucien?"

He cleared his throat and began to fidget with his t-shirt. Looking down, he began. "Isabella, I know why I am the way I am, why I do the things I do."

She said nothing in response, only waited for him to continue.

"I only waited this long to tell you so I knew you would be ready, or at least, I think you are," he said. "My mother told me I am… not really a human."

"So what are you, Lucien?" Isabella asked quietly, the light smile fading from her lips.

He was still for a moment. "I am a cross between a witch and a vampire."

Isabella smiled once again and looked back at the sky.

Lucien continued. "She only waited so long to tell me because she said I am the first and only one of my kind. She said she had to watch me because no one knew what to expect."

"I guess that tells you a lot, huh?" Isabella continued to gaze at the stars.

She nodded. "Yeah, I guess so."

The two teenagers were quiet for a moment, then Isabella began to speak. "I have a confession to make, Lucien."

The boy only looked at her, waiting patiently for her to continue. "I am not human either. At least, not fully."

Now she had his full attention, and he even turned his body in her direction, waiting anxiously. "What do you mean?"

"My parents told me last week. They said I am a vampire also, at least half. My mother was human when she had me, but she is a vampire now, too. I am part human." She turned and looked at him. "Lucien, everyone in the world is a vampire, and we are all part of the same Family, they said. It is important that we come to see this and accept it. That is the only way you can ever be the Master your father would have wanted."

At first, he was tempted to get angry with Isabella for keeping all of this to herself. If her parents had talked to her last week, why had she not brought that information to him? Then he reasoned with himself; he had hidden similar information from her for months. They both held on to the secret for their own time. He had no room to be angry with her.

"They also told me about you, and they told me you knew," she said. "I was just waiting for you to be ready to talk to me about it. I hope you see the greatness you have been destined for because I see it. This is why you must control your... our... urges, Lucien."

Isabella paused for a bit before continuing. "My parents also told me that the gods created me to be your wife. I am destined for you, the perfect bride for a perfect Master. I am not afraid because I know the Family needs a strong Master, and I know you need a strong wife, Lucien."

Now the two looked at each other in silence. There was a stillness in both of their eyes that brought peace to each of them. The acceptance they felt for each other was tangible, and both Lucien and Isabella knew that all of this was meant to be. All of it, from their individual species to their future together. It was intentional, orchestrated by whoever was really in charge of this planet and everyone on it.

As they looked into each other's eyes, Lucien was overcome with the desire to kiss Isabella, softly, but with passion. He had never felt such love and belonging as he was experiencing that moment, and he wanted it to last. He leaned forward slowly, afraid of making her nervous or scaring her off, but she simply sat still and smiled. Yes, they had kissed before, but it had been childish experimentation. Now Lucien's heart was pounding, and he felt longings that were very adult in nature.

His lips met hers as lightly as if a feather was brushing her mouth. The two simply held their lips together, not moving at all. Then Lucien opened his mouth slightly, and Isabella responded in kind. Soon he had his hand tangled in her hair, and his kisses became more passionate. Their tongues touched, and they tasted each other's lips. Lucien could feel his penis growing as hard as a rock inside of his jeans, and it was becoming quite uncomfortable.

"Isabella, I…" he began, but she pulled away and put her forefinger to his lips to quiet him. She turned and looked at the house behind her. It was all lit up, but there was no sign of Patrick or Rose.

She turned back to him. "Let's go to my treehouse," she said with a whisper.

Lucien nodded as Isabella took his hand. They stood and began walking to the backyard, where her treehouse was snuggly perched in a massive oak, a good distance from the house. They climbed the ladder that ran up the tree trunk, and once they were inside, Isabella turned on an electric lantern which served as a wonderful source of soft light. She then opened a pink trunk that sat next to a little table, and out of it, she pulled a teal sleeping bag. How many times the two of them had used that sleeping bag to keep warm while looking at the stars could not be counted.

Now Isabella spread it over the floor of the treehouse, and she sat down on it, watching Lucien closely. After a moment, he rose and took his place beside her. Their lips met once again, but this time their hands began to explore each other's bodies slowly, but with great interest. To both Lucien and Isabella it was right; it was time.

Lucien's hand went timidly to Isabella's breast; he expected her to become uncomfortable or panic. He felt overwhelmed by his nerves, so she had to be as well, but she surprised him, however, as she leaned into his touch. For a fleeting moment, Lucien found himself wondering if her parents had prepared her for this as well. If almost seemed as though both of them were under the control of some unseen force, and it felt completely natural.

He felt her small, hard nipple with his thumb, and it made him draw in a sharp breath. Isabella leaned away from him and stood. She began to take her clothes off, and he saw the first bit of nervousness in her eyes. He smiled comfortingly at her, and she smiled back.

Isabella was a virgin, but she knew that this night was to be. Her inexperience had her stomach in knots; never before had anyone touched her in this way, and even though it was destined, she had to fight off the desire to say no and make him stop. After all, both of them were only thirteen. She wanted to do it, her body wanted to do it, but her young mind wanted to fight the process. She forced her body to submit and even respond to the fumbling touches of her young future husband.

Lucien was indeed fumbling, and even in his inexperience, he was aware of it. Oh, yes, all of this was meant to be, but what were they both doing, did they really even know? He loved girls, the way they looked, felt, and smelled, especially his Isabella, but it was this fact that made him even more nervous. What if she laughed at his apparent clumsiness?

He pushed his thoughts out of his mind and looked at her in the dim light. Her naked body was perfect to Lucien, even at her young age. He had seen plenty of naked girls in the magazines that he had stolen from Martin Lamb and kept hidden in his secret spot. Isabella was not as ripe as some of them, but she certainly would be. His penis was so hard he thought it would burst if he continued to look at her and touch her. He wanted to know what she felt like, so he tore his eyes from her.

He stood as well and soon both of them were completely bare. They looked at each other for only a moment before Lucien approached her and began to kiss her again. Their bodies brushed together as they kissed, and the feeling of Isabella's hard nipples was driving him out of his mind. He could feel her trembling, and he knew then that she was as anxious about what they were going to do as he was.

"Don't be scared, Isabella," Lucien whispered to her.

She blushed slightly and smiled, looking at the floor. "I can't help it. I am pretty sure it is normal for the first time."

Lucien leaned forward and kissed her on the forehead, then planted light kisses down each side of her face before softly planting his lips on hers. Her tiny tongue darted into his mouth, and he caught it and sucked on it gently. She tasted sweet, like candy. He wondered what the rest of her body would taste like to him.

Lucien put his hand on the back of her head and held her tightly to him as he kissed her. He could handle it for only a few seconds, though. He knew that any moment he was going to make a mess all over the front of her belly, and he did not want to embarrass either of them that way. He pulled away from her and sat on the blanket, taking her hand and gently pulling her down after him. Soon, they were lying on the sleeping bag on their sides. Isabella could feel his hard penis brushing against her legs and lower belly. It made her stomach shake, but she could hardly wait to show him how much she loved him by giving her body to him completely.

Lucien kept kissing her, steering her onto her back. Soon he was on top of her, and even though he knew what to do next, he hesitated. This was Isabella, after all, and he didn't want to hurt her. He had read that it hurt girls the first time. He could not bear the thought of being the one to cause her any kind of pain, no matter how natural the pain was.

Suddenly, Isabella jerked forward onto him, and before he even knew what had happened, he was inside of her. She let out a tiny cry of pain as her virginity was captured by him. So tight she was down there, Lucien was thinking. He doubted very highly that this, their first time having sex, was going to last very long at all.

Soon, they were both moving feverishly against each other, and in only a few thrusts, Lucien lost control, his body rigid and frozen. As inexperienced as she was, Isabella continued to move her hips against him. All she knew was that it felt like the right thing to do, and Lucien was so grateful she did. He couldn't move as his body released his seed into his young lover.

Finally, he collapsed on top of her, his body spent. Wow, he had never felt anything like that in his entire life! All of a sudden the existence of Martin Lamb's magazines in the world made sense, as did all the sounds he had heard coming from his mother's quarters over the years.

Isabella stroked his hair and his back as they lay together. She did not want to rush the moment. She wasn't sure why, but something inside of her told her this act was going to change things, at least for a while. She didn't know what that meant, and she didn't want to think about it.

After a bit, Lucien rose up on his elbows. They looked at each other in the dim light, and both of them burst out laughing; the children in them came out. He rolled off of her, and they lay naked together holding hands, comfortable and content.

He turned to her, his thumb stroking hers. "Are you okay? Did it hurt too much?"

"No," she replied. "Only a bit, and only for a second."

Lucien rolled over on his side and got up on his elbow so he could look down at her. "Did it feel as good for you as it did for me?"

"Well," she began. "It felt good, but from the way you acted, it was likely not the same. Maybe the next time it will be. It is probably because it was my first time."

He nodded and lay back down. "Maybe," he said.

"I love you, Lucien," Isabella said quietly.

Lucien took in a deep breath. "I think I love you too, Isabella."

∞

At the exact same moment that Lucien and Isabella were consummating their love for the very first time, Patrick looked up at Rose from the book he was reading. She looked up at him as well, and they both smiled.

"It is done," Patrick said softly.

Rose nodded and smiled. "Yes," she replied before looking back down at her knitting.

Patrick had never liked the idea, but he knew it was beyond his control. He sat back in his chair, his book open in his hands. He was much calmer now that it was over, the Powers would be pleased with them all.

Rasia called them the 'Powers' as if she knew them personally, and Patrick did not understand that, but he was certain it had something to do with her being part witch. He thought that witches had a different understanding of the Powers than what he originally felt with Cyril's power. When Cyril had made the Queen and Rasia fully changed, the Powers were all so clear to all the family shifting from Cyril to a much higher power. It didn't matter to Patrick what they were called; to him, they were one and the same.

He stood and put his book face down on his desk. "I suppose we should turn in. I don't want to embarrass the girl when she finally decides to come in. Let's let them be."

Rose nodded and put her knitting into the basket beside her chair. She stood and took her husband's hand, and together they went to their chambers. It was time to turn in. They didn't need to be concerned about Isabella anymore. Tonight she had become a woman, and no matter how uneasy the details made her parents, they both knew it was something they would have to live with, if not learn to love.

∞

Lucien and Isabella dressed and stayed in the treehouse talking for the next two hours. They did not discuss having sex together, they talked only about Lucien's anger toward Rasia. It was an anger that seemed to have a mind of its own, at least in Isabella's opinion. She found herself concerned about what Lucien might eventually do to his own mother, but she kept her worries to herself.

When he finally got ready to leave, the two kissed each other softly goodbye, and he walked her to her front door. There they parted ways, Isabella to the comfort of her bed, and Lucien to go home to the massive, lonely White House. He thought about the love he and Isabella had made only until he arrived at his front door, then all thoughts of the incident left his mind.

He showered and climbed between his sheets, and he lay there in the darkness thinking. Suddenly he found himself considering women in general. What did Stella, the head of their servants, look like without her clothes on? What about his mother? Were they as tempting and luscious as Isabella had been? What did they smell like up close? He knew now that Isabella's scent had become extremely powerful when her skin was right under his nose. Before he had showered, he could smell her all over him, and even now the memory of her scent and the feel of her body on the inside was giving him another erection.

But the actual girl he had just been with was now the furthest thing from Lucien's mind. He found himself obsessing over every woman he had ever encountered over his lifetime, though they had been few. He knew that, for the time being at least, he would not be satisfied to just have Isabella. He wanted to sample each and every one. He wanted to smell them, taste their flesh, and feel them from the inside, as he had done earlier tonight.

Yes, suddenly he was not concerned with his girl Isabella at all.

∞

Isabella was lying with her eyes closed, and she could not stop thinking about Lucien. It had been magic, what the two of them had done tonight. She found she was more devoted to him than ever.

But something tugged at her heart. She knew that it was not going to be easy for some reason. She felt like the sex had been a catalyst of sorts, and she felt confusion and fear with that knowledge.

All she could do was be patient and steadfast. Her father and mother told her that when something was meant to be, one had to wait for it to come full circle. One could not get distracted or give up, losing focus.

Finally, she fell into a fitful sleep, filled with uncomfortable dreams that she wouldn't remember when she woke.

R.W.K. Clark

CHAPTER 13

Lucien walked into the dining room the next morning in a state of complete distraction. It seemed he could suddenly smell every woman in the house, and while it was pleasant, it made him feel a sense of powerlessness he was not accustomed to. A servant had walked by him upstairs in the hall carrying a pile of sheets, and for the first time, the woman stared at him, even following him with her eyes. She had even smiled flirtatiously. Was it all in his head? For Lucien, it was all he could do to keep from throwing her on the floor and ravaging her.

Lack of self-control wouldn't do now; he had come way too far. Now that he knew who he was and what his future really held he was determined not to ruin it. He would find another way to indulge his sexual fantasies, one that wouldn't put his future at risk.

His mother was already seated before her breakfast. Lucien sat at the far end of the long table, as far from her as he could get. He hadn't sat close to her, except during lesson time, since their confrontation on his birthday.

"Good morning," she said to him as he sat.

He nodded in response and unfolded his napkin, placing it on his lap. He then rang the bell a single time to let the kitchen staff know he had arrived, then he looked at his mother. She smiled at him, but he did not smile back.

Rasia cleared her throat. "So, the Powers have let me know that they have sealed the relationship you have with Isabella."

Now she had his attention. He looked her in the eyes, but he refused to speak. He didn't need to if the witch already knew so much.

"You do realize that you will both be married someday," she said. "But I also know that right now Isabella is not even in your thoughts. That is normal."

Lucien remained silent. He was more concerned about listening to every word the woman had to say. He had much to learn, and it was vital that he begin learning his lessons well.

"Regardless, you will enter a very… physical phase in your life," she told him. "It may be hard to understand, especially for Isabella, but you will both eventually get through it. I expect you to handle yourself responsibly during this time. No killing of Family."

He wanted to ask her what she meant exactly, but something inside of him already knew. The strong, constant stirring in his groin that had arrived last night was explanation enough. As for Isabella, he knew she wasn't going anywhere. She would be fine regardless of what he chose to do, and he knew that very well.

Rasia took a bite of her food and chewed it up,

swallowing it daintily. "I will be going to New York to tend to some business at Cliffside. I will be gone for a week. You are a man now," she reminded him. "I expect that you will handle things the right way here. Martin will be with me, so you are in charge."

A female servant appeared carrying Lucien's breakfast. As she put his plate before him, her scent filled his nose, and a low growl escaped his throat. The girl turned to him and smiled, then she gave him a quick wink before returning to the kitchen.

Lucien was in shock. Had that woman just winked at him? Had his mother taken notice of the exchange? He looked up at her; she sat looking at him. A sly, knowing smile on her face.

"As I was saying, it is essential that you be the very picture of responsibility, Lucien," she continued, still smiling with obvious amusement. "Do you understand what I am saying, or do I need to elaborate?"

He shook his head. "Good, I didn't want to have to go into all the gory details. It has always been your strongest traits, your insight, and intelligence."

Rasia rose, wiping her lips on her napkin. "I need to be going. The plane is already waiting. I will see you when I return." With that, she left the room. No affection, no hugging. There never was, and Lucien hated her for that as well.

He ate his breakfast quickly and went to his room. He had a lot to think about, and he needed to be alone to do it. No distractions, he just wanted to sort things out in his head.

Shortly after he lay down, the telephone rang next to his bed. He looked over at the caller id display: Isabella. He did not want to talk to her now. He had way too much on his mind. He let the phone ring until it stopped, then he turned the ringer off. The servants knew not to answer their private phone. He felt better now.

Lucien focused on all that was new that day, from the loss of his virginity to feeling compelled to have sex again as soon as possible. How was he to deal with that? He may be officially a 'man,' but he was still thirteen. The stirring between his legs and the nagging in his mind would drive him mad if he didn't find a way to quiet them both.

His first opportunity came later that afternoon, much to his shock and surprise. He had completely lost track of time lying on his bed. He had even been fantasizing about sex, imaging some of the things he would do the next time he had an opportunity to be alone with a woman. The smell of the women downstairs was trickling under his door, driving him mad.

He was tossing and turning, wide awake when he heard a light knocking at his bedroom door. "Yes?" he questioned sternly.

The door opened slowly, and a petite blond servant poked her head inside. "Master Lucien?"

He sat up on the edge of his bed. "Yes?"

Now the girl became bolder. She opened the door all the way and stepped inside, and though she kept her head slightly bowed out of respect, she looked him in the eye. She was pretty, with her hair pulled up and tiny ringlets hanging around her face. Her blue eyes seemed to be lit up brightly.

"I just wanted to know if there is... anything... I can do for you," she said coyly, a smile playing on her lips.

The woman was flirting with him, and the smell of her desire was coming off of her in great waves. It was making him dizzy, and he was having a hard time understanding what was happening. Was this woman in his room to... seduce him?

Lucien chose his words carefully. "Are you here for my laundry?"

She shook her head and then looked behind her into the hall. When she saw it was empty, she entered his room all the way and closed the door behind her. "I am here for anything you want or need, Master."

Now Lucien stood, filled with confidence he was not accustomed to. He walked over to her and stood before her, looking at her face. They were the same height, and his direct stare seemed to intimidate her. Her eyes fell to the floor.

He lifted his hand and touched her face. "What is your name?"

The girl continued to look at the floor. "Amanda."

He stroked her cheek with his thumb. "Amanda," he said, tasting her name on his lips.

Lucien leaned forward then and covered her mouth with his own. She tasted of mint and blood; she had fed today, and the flavor proved to drive him even harder. He grabbed her arms and pulled her to him, and she did not put up a fight. Soon they were ripping at each other's clothing, ripping the cloth and shredding the items until they fell to the floor.

Lucien was determined to taste her, and without revealing his intent, he put her to the floor quickly. She lay down in submission, spreading her legs to receive him, but he buried his face there instead. Suddenly Lucien knew he had found heaven.

He indulged himself with this woman in this way for nearly an hour, and she was all too eager. She moaned and squirmed in a manner that drove him out of his mind, but he did not lose control this time. After he had had enough, he mounted her and thrust his young manhood deep inside of her, then he slowed himself down. He was going to enjoy this.

He did her with long, languid strokes, and she clawed at his back and hair as he did. When he could take no more, he picked up the pace, and Amanda met him stroke for stroke with her hips. He burst violently inside of her, and they both cried out.

They lay on the floor next to each other in silence, Lucien replaying the entire scene over and over in his mind. Already he wanted more. Suddenly his mind flashed to Isabella, and he jumped up.

"You should go," he said stiffly. "I have things to do today."

Amanda stood and gathered the rags that were once her uniform. "If you ever want me…"

"We'll see," he said and turned to his dresser for fresh clothing. He chose his items and turned his back to her, hoping she would get the hint.

After a time she finally did, and she turned and left the room. Where she went or what she did, mattered not to Lucien, he just wanted her gone. He was finished with that one. He pulled his jeans on, then a clean t-shirt. He could smell the woman on his face, and all it proved to do was make him wonder who the next one would be.

The thought of Isabella had left his mind as quickly as it had come. He was not even aware of his lack of concern for the girl. All he felt right now was hunger. He glanced at the clock and saw that he was past due for his lunch. He smiled and left his room.

He hoped they made chili dogs for him.

∞

The next six months proved to be a very painful and trying time for Isabella Gilliam.

Lucien had immediately become distant after their first sexual encounter. He hardly answered her calls, and on more than one occasion, he canceled plans for her to visit. She felt the distance between them, and it was like a massive gap in her world that led to nothing but a dark abyss. She didn't understand what was happening, and she cried herself to sleep constantly over it.

She suspected he didn't love her anymore, and that was the change she had felt take place when they were done having sex. At least, she assumed that was so. Lucien did not approach her to make love again during this time, and she was heartbroken. She took her pains to her mother.

"I don't understand, mum," she began, large tears falling from her eyes. "He doesn't even want to see me."

Rose and Isabella were in the girl's room sitting on the bed. Rose rubbed her daughter's shoulders as she cried. She knew what was happening, and she felt that now was the time to tell her everything about this relationship. If she did not, Isabella might not stick it out and fulfill her true destiny with Lucien.

She allowed the girl to cry until her tears were spent. She took a handkerchief and wiped the girl's face, then took her by the arms and straightened her out, turning her to face her. She lifted Isabella's chin with a single finger, making her look her in the eye.

"I have some things to tell you, dear," she began.

Isabella looked at her mother expectantly, her eyes intent and wide. "As a male of the species, Lucien will go through certain… changes that you won't go through," Rose began.

"What kind of changes?" Isabella asked.

Rose was not sure how to proceed. "I am going to get your father. He can explain this as I cannot. Wait here." She stood and left the room quickly.

Isabella wrung her hands, her brow creased and her stomach trembled. Had she been wrong all along? Was the relationship she had imagined her and Lucien to have her entire life nothing but a pipe dream, a fantasy? She began to breathe deeply, calming herself for her parents.

After only a minute, Rose and Patrick came into the room. Now Patrick sat beside his daughter. He draped his arm across her shoulders and pulled her to him, giving her a gentle hug before sitting her right and looking at her.

"Isabella, what you and Lucien did on your birthday was inevitable, I want you to rest assured of that," he began. "With that being said, Lucien is male. In vampires, this means that once sexual relations have been initiated, the male of the species becomes hyper-aware of other females for an extended period of time."

Patrick watched his daughter closely as he spoke; this helped him weigh his words properly. Now her beautiful face was calm. He knew she was listening, and he trusted her maturity level enough to know she would take all he said to heart.

"Lucien will not be able to control this; it is the nature of this beast," he continued in a matter-of-fact tone. "He will be engaging in sexual activity with virtually every female he comes into contact with, and you should also know that they will be pulled to him. They will both be powerless."

"So what you're saying is that Lucien is going to have other girlfriends?" Tears were pooling up in Isabella's eyes, and her breathing was becoming rapid.

Patrick took hold of her arm to calm her. "No, what I am saying is that he will have sex with other girls and women, Isabella. He will grow out of it. Understand that clearly!"

A confused look came over her face. "He'll be having sex, but they won't be his girlfriends?"

"Dear, take our dog Chester for example. He chases female dogs, does he not? The part of Lucien that will be engaging in this will be the animal, the vampire." Patrick took her hand. "The two of you will be together. It has been marked in the annals of all time. But for now, you must keep that knowledge in the forefront of your mind. Do not let yourself or your emotions shake you. You must remain his and his alone. You cannot afford to be distracted."

"What should I do?" she asked.

He smiled gently. "Take the time away from him that you need. Put this all together in your mind; organize it. Take six months or a year. Then you will see because he knows you are his destiny as well."

Isabella took a deep breath and squared her shoulders. "I think I understand. I'm going to make a line between us, but not one that can never be erased." She wiped at her eyes. "I want to be alone for a while. I will decide how to tell him later."

Rose now approached her daughter and began to stroke her hair. "We are here, Isabella, anytime you need to talk. Do you want us to tell him?"

"No," she replied with determination. "It's my responsibility." Isabella lay down on her bed and turned to face the wall.

Patrick took Rose by the arm, and they left the room silently, closing the door behind him. Patrick said, "She will be fine. She is strong like diamonds, and she understands what has to be."

"I just wish she would let us talk to him for her," Rose said. "I've never fully trusted Lucien. What if he becomes enraged?"

Patrick smiled and shook his head. "No. He has barely thought of her since this has taken over. Give it time; it will come back to him as he grows stronger and begins to gain control over his own instincts."

∞

Lucien stared at the caller id unit. Isabella was calling, and while he didn't want to talk to her, something told him to answer it. He lifted the receiver slowly. "Hello?"

"Hi, Lucien," Isabella began. "You don't have to say anything. I just wanted to call you and tell you that we need to take some time apart."

"Okay."

Isabella fought back the tears his callousness had caused. She cleared her throat and said, "Okay, so maybe we'll run into each other sometime. Take care of yourself."

She quickly hung up the phone and buried her face in her pillow. She sobbed into the pillow, muffling her cries so her parents wouldn't hear. Once she was spent, she reached over and turned the ringer off on her phone. Isabella sat up on the edge of her bed and shook it off; being with Lucien was not going to be her reality right now, and she was going to accept it.

With that, she stood and went to the bathroom to shower. It would be time for supper soon, and maybe her parents would want to watch a movie.

Life would go on. No matter how she felt or how much the rejection she was experiencing dominated her heart and her thoughts, life would go on. It was time for Isabella Gilliam to forget about her lifelong love, Lucien DeSai, for a long, long while.

∞

Lucien stared at the telephone receiver gripped in his hand. Isabella cut him off quick, and it made something echo of pain in his chest, but it was so, so faint. It was best this way, and they both knew it. He hung up the telephone and looked out the window at the sparkling night.

A single tear fell from his eye. He quickly wiped it away, and he did not shed another. He had quite a bit of living to do and crying like a girl was not the way to begin.

CHAPTER 14

Festival des Ames, or the Festival of Souls, was a yearly celebration that took place all around the world. Every member of the Family, man, woman, and child, took two full days to do nothing but play, and no form of play was barred. Rasia founded the festival, which paid homage to the Powers with sacrifices that included feasting bloody food and drinking the very best blood, served by those who had stockpiled donations left before Cyril had come. Sexual orgies and a bit of playful violence were always to be expected.

No Family member ever tried to 'duck out' of recognizing Festival des Ames. To do so would incur great consequences, and besides, it was far too much fun. It was the highlight of the year.

Isabella would be going to this one alone. It had been eleven months since she had seen or talked to Lucien, and the last festival had been twelve months ago. She would attend it without male companionship, but she would be sociable and hold her head high.

There would be a local gathering in each city, town, and village worldwide. She was dressed and ready to go to the gathering. It was at the Capitol building, and it would be a crazy time. She wanted to take advantage of this opportunity to loosen up. Since Lucien, she had become somewhat of a recluse, but no more.

She had poured herself into her studies, and it had paid off. At fourteen, she was preparing to graduate, and mother and father were taking advantage of the services of the local college. She would live at home, and her studies would be sent to her. Lectures would be watched via satellite, and she would be able to participate along with the rest of the class. She was very excited.

The entire world knew what Lucien was doing and what he was enduring. He was suddenly "Master' to everyone, and the Family's knowledge of his role made him the focal point of everyone's life. She was embarrassed, and she didn't want to hear it all the time. This was why she had opted to study from home.

She was biding her time.

Now she was looking at herself in the mirror. She knew how beautiful she was, but she had a humble soul, and the two played together perfectly. Her high intelligence made her a shoo-in when she encountered people who took her for a 'dumb blonde.' She was anything but.

The fact was she knew how to carry herself. She knew what she was, and she wore it with grace. Isabella Gilliam was indeed a diamond, but she was in love with someone who was still a chunk of coal.

She ran her hands down her form-fitting sapphire blue silk dress. She wore white satin gloves with no fingertips, which allowed her to show off her gorgeous manicure. She sucked in her breath, hoping she didn't see Lucien there tonight.

Well, I do not have time for crying and the like, she thought. Mom and Dad are waiting. It was time to enjoy the Festival of Souls.

∞

Music without rhyme or rhythm was blaring through the night sky. It was filled with guttural groans and random screams, and people writhed to its sound. Others chatted loudly, speaking over one another and holding their drinks high to avoid them spilling.

It was beautiful chaos.

A smile spread across Isabella's lips. It occurred to her that this was only her second time coming to the Festival. Her parents and Rasia had not even told them it existed. Both she and Lucien had been confined to their respective homes each year on this night for their own protection. Now she knew what she was and could participate, and she didn't have Lucien to drag her down. She began to feel a new sense of hope.

For the first hour, she was there, Isabella was a social butterfly. She met all the girls she could around her age, and she blended into their company beautifully. She laughed, made jokes, and even indulged in a bit of intellectual conversation here and there.

Everything was wonderful, then she heard her name being called sharply by some woman behind her. The sound of the voice was not pleasant. "Isabella!"

She looked over one shoulder and then the other.

To her right, stood a busty blond woman with a small waist and wide hips. The dress she wore was too tight, and she had on too much makeup. Isabella would have guessed she was about twenty, but as she continued to look at her, she realized the girl was probably closer to sixteen.

The girl was smiling a nasty smile at Isabella, then she jerked her head over her left shoulder. Isabella followed the gesture, and there stood Lucien, his black eyes smoldering with the fire of anger. The woman simply said, "Need I say more?"

Isabella couldn't help but smile. This woman was loud, brash, and displayed no class whatsoever. She looked at Lucien and, smiling, said, "I hope you and your date are enjoying your night."

Lucien, whose arm was being held by the girl, jerked away from her violently. The crowd around them grew completely still, and the silence seemed to spread.

"How dare you!" He growled at the girl. "How dare you presume to interfere in my life? I just scraped you off the street and brought you here. You are nothing!"

He swung and hit her in the face with the back of his hand. She fell backward into the crowd, blood flying.

Isabella did nothing. She simply turned back to the woman she had been talking to and resumed her conversation, her back to Lucien. She heard him growling and yelling as he stormed off through the crowd.

Isabella continued to talk as if nothing had happened. She felt an odd mixture of sadness and satisfaction. Yes, it was better this way for now.

∞

Something was happening. Lucien didn't know what, but something was happening.

He lay on his bed, still in the suit he had worn to the Festival. That stupid witch! Who did she think she was to go anywhere near his Isabella and draw attention to herself? He had intended to ravage the daylights out of her, but when he saw her behavior, he had been sickened by it. Now his night was ruined.

But not just because he did not get laid, he could do that still. It was just that something about it did not appeal to him. Something to do with Isabella.

He hardly thought of her anymore, even though he seemed constantly aware of her existence. Tonight she saw him with that broad, and he could see her eyes light up. He knew he looked good for a fourteen-year-old. But she had also looked... amused.

It was humiliating. She saw him for what he was and what he had become, he knew that. He did nothing but scrounge for women, day after day. It was like a light turned on in his mind, and he was suddenly aware of how much of an animal the satisfying of his instincts actually made him.

But even as he thought about the truth, he felt his loins stir, and Isabella disappeared from his mind like a puff of smoke. He stood and looked himself over in the mirror. The last year had brought about many physical changes for him. His hair was long, full, and silky. It was black as pitch. He also had a bit of facial hair, and he had a beautifully structured body.

They came in droves, the women did, and suddenly he knew he had to pick himself up. He freshened up a bit and then trotted down the stairs. He had barely opened the door when two women appeared out of nowhere, laughing and waving drinks.

Lucien opened the door wide to grant them access. He shut the door behind them and locked it, smiling. Once again, Isabella ceased to exist to him, if only for a time.

CHAPTER 15

Isabella flipped a switch in her mind, and it turned Lucien off.

She was not angry with him or even hurt, for that matter. Seeing him standing there with that nasty, rude girl had been the best thing that could have happened. It showed her how low his sexual instincts would take him. She knew right then she wasn't dealing with Lucien, she was dealing with the vampire inside.

Her father told her it would pass, and she knew deep inside that it would. He simply needed to grow into his sexual identity, and she needed only to focus and wait. She was willing to do both, and so she flipped that switch.

Now, it was nearly seven months since the Festival, and Isabella was well into her first year of college studies, and things were going perfectly. She had begun to make a few friends, and Lucien was not the focal point of her life. She was going to study history as a major, only because she could, and it interested her greatly. She was content and satisfied.

Boys would flirt with her over the television screen which assisted her in attending classes from home, and a couple had even crowded the camera and asked her out. She had been tempted on both occasions, but apologetically refused. She had too much on her plate, she told them.

Both times, she found herself feeling melancholy for the rest of the day. She wanted to date and get to know others. She longed for sex, and she thought about it often, even satisfying herself frequently. It sometimes wasn't fair, but it was what it was.

Now she was going to be fifteen very soon. She hoped he would come around sooner than later. It would have been nice to have him over for her birthday. Sometimes she missed him terribly, especially during their birthday celebrations.

∞

Lucien sat naked on the edge of his bed, his head in his hands. He had just rid himself of his latest conquest. He couldn't wait to be rid of her! Only this one and one other, about a month ago, had this effect on him and it confused him. Never, outside of those two, had he felt such disgust toward the female of the species.

He rose and went to shower. He didn't want to smell her on him anymore He was anxious to clean up and find the next so he could feel better. He hated the empty feeling that had been left behind.

When he was clean and dressed, he went downstairs and grabbed a bite to eat from the refrigerator in the dark, empty kitchen. Everyone had gone home for the night. He had hoped to maybe use the services of one of the maids, but no one was to be found.

He made a ham and Swiss cheese sandwich and leaned against the counter to eat it. While he chewed, he began to feel like staying home. Maybe it would be good to just get a satisfying night's rest.

Suddenly his mind flashed to Isabella. He wondered what she would be doing this night. The thought of her made something ache inside of him, something strange, yet familiar. The memory of her silky blond hair came to mind, and he winced with pain. What was this all about?

Lucien had not seen Isabella since the Festival, and that had been months ago. She had come to mind twice since, and the emotions he felt both times had grown stronger. His brow creased with concern.

He finished his sandwich and washed it down with water. Yes, he needed sleep. He had obviously deprived himself of sleep lately, and these crazy thoughts would be remedied by a good sleep. He took off his clean jacket and swung it over his shoulder and walked back to his room.

He stripped down and got under the covers. His mind went to sex immediately. He thought about a faceless blond woman with her legs spread out before him. In his fantasy, he was biting at her and licking her nipples, making his way down her belly. Right before he dove in, he looked up to see her expression, and it was the face of Isabella.

Lucien sat up straight in the darkroom and stared straight ahead, his heart pounding. He wanted her off his mind! He had become accustomed to her absence, and now all of these recollected memories were causing him massive amounts of grief and distraction. This was not part of the plan he had made for himself in the last eighteen months or so. What was he going to do to rid himself of them? Lucien rocked a bit on the side of his bed as he thought about a solution, but when none came to him, he fell back into his pillow in frustration, praying that sleep would come.

Finally, he dozed off, but he spent the night tossing and turning, Isabella dancing through his dreams, her blond hair blowing in an unfelt breeze.

CHAPTER 16

Rasia had been watching her son very, very closely, and she was pleased with what she saw.

Lucien was coming along into his manhood just as expected. She had been very worried about this period of his life; other men in the Family had educated her as to how it was, and with the knowledge of his lineage, she was right to be concerned. She had been fully prepared to find bodies strewn all over the place while he grew into himself.

But it never happened, and now he was on the downhill slope of his change. He was fifteen, and according to the others, he would be completely through this phase of his growth by sixteen, or shortly after at the latest.

His behavior was changing as well, and this was the surest sign in her mind. He wasn't prowling so much, to begin with. That was the first sign she had been told to look for. Now he was going out only four or five times a week as opposed to several times a night, and the women? In the beginning, she would see countless females leaving at all hours of the night. In the last few months, she would remember a total of only ten or twelve.

Lucien's mood had also become calmer, almost morose. He was often quiet and deep in thought. She often asked if he needed a listening ear, but he would growl and storm off. Rasia knew he had to work through the changes on his own.

She fully expected him to come to her in the next year or so, though, and speak to her about Isabella. Rasia thought that the girl's absence was beginning to come to mind, meaning he was breaking, though. If this were the case, he would want to know how to deal with the situation. She was ready to help if he came to her for guidance. In the meantime, she would wait patiently, just as she knew Isabella had done and was still doing. It would all come full circle.

∞

Lucien's mother was correct when she noted that his drive was diminishing. He knew that she was always watching him, and he could almost read her mind, or so it seemed. Yes, the women were becoming a bit more burdensome and boring than before, and oftentimes he was angry with himself when he was finished with one. Something about what he was doing didn't seem... right. Not the physical part, but all that went with it.

He pushed those thoughts far from his mind as soon as they came, but when he did he would then see Isabella in his mind's eye, and the vision almost made him nauseous. Why he wasn't sure. He just knew his feelings toward all this sex were changing. Perhaps he was simply experiencing boredom.

They weren't changing enough to stop him fully, though. He often would go back into the obsessive mindset, but it always went away, and he found himself here, reclining in his room, staring at the ceiling, almost depressed. It felt like an impossible situation.

Yes, Rasia was right. But one thing she didn't know, one thing that had escaped her, was that often Lucien was thinking about ending her. Those were the times when he would growl at her interruptions. He felt stronger than ever now, and so did the hatred he felt for that despicable woman. He knew deep inside that the day was fast approaching when he would get the job done, and he often daydreamed and fantasized about it to get his mind off Isabella.

He was fifteen now, and he had much more confidence in who he was and what he would be. It was just a matter of time before he took his place at the head of the Family, and the thought excited him. The world and everything in it was to be his. He just wasn't sure what he wanted to do with it yet.

Oh, well, he thought. It will come to me.

∞

Isabella received a letter.

Her mother had let her know it when she came to her study room to get her for lunch. "You have mail, dear. When you are finished, you can grab it from the hall."

"Thanks," she replied. She was starved, and she tore into her food with gusto. Her mother sat across from her and ate with her usual lady-like grace.

"It's from Rasia DeSai," she said softly.

Isabella stopped eating and looked at her mother. "What do you suppose it is?" she asked.

Rose shrugged and put her fork down on her plate. "I assume it is an invitation to Lucien's sixteenth birthday in three months. Rasia will be getting a head start on this one; it's important."

Now it was Isabella's turn to put her fork down. "Why would she invite me? I don't want to go."

Now Rose's voice took on a stern quality. "It's time, Isabella."

The girl only shook her head defiantly. "I do not want to go. I'm happy, Mother. Maybe I don't want to change things now."

"There is no choice, and you know it."

Isabella looked down at the plate of food on the table, tears forming in her eyes. She knew the day would eventually come, but she wasn't' ready for it now. She had friends. She had her own life! Time had passed, and things were in her favor. How dare Rasia or Lucien think it was okay to assume she still wanted him?

Rose continued. "You still have three months to reconcile yourself to the fact. Lucien has grown strong. He is seeing things more clearly now, as a man sees."

"Excuse me," Isabella said as she stood from the table. "I need some time alone."

Rose nodded. "Take the mail you have with you."

Isabella walked out of the room and grabbed the envelope from the hall table, crumpling it in her hand. It was still firmly in her grasp when she threw herself on her bed. She closed her eyes and breathed in and out, preparing to open the letter.

After a bit, she held the envelope up and straightened it a bit. Rasia's distinctive writing graced the paper, and Isabella felt a tug of bittersweet at seeing it. Rasia had always been very good to her, and their relationship had definitely been their own. Even though she hadn't seen much of the woman since Lucien had changed, she still felt a great affection for her, and even missed her greatly at times.

Isabella ran her fingers over the front of the envelope, thinking hard about the inevitable events to come. She had always been so determined to get through this and come into her rightful place with Lucien. She never expected to feel the way she was feeling. She had come into her own, and she had put a lot of work into sparing her own heart. Now it was as if none of that mattered. She was expected to step up with a smile on her face, and that fact was both frustrating and infuriating. How dare they?

The truth that she knew well was that her emotions were emanating from the human part of her, the part that was susceptible to feeling. She would not put up a fight, and she knew it. She would work through this and do exactly what she was expected to do, what she was meant to do.

After a while, Isabella sat up on the edge of her bed and tore the corner off the envelope. She then slid her finger inside and tore the flap open. She withdrew a very beautiful card with words of gold embossed calligraphy on cream cardstock. Rasia was really going all out for Lucien's sixteenth birthday celebration. It seemed as if she were as relieved that Lucien was coming around as Isabella probably should have been.

The card cordially invited her and her parents to Lucien's celebration dinner and subsequent party. It would be small, the announcement promised, with only Lucien, Rasia, and the Gilliams, if they would be so kind as to come, in attendance. Isabella knew that meant Martin Lamb as well, and she could only assume this was so reconciliation could properly take place.

She opened the invitation slowly, and a folded piece of stationery fell out and fluttered to the floor. She stared at it for several minutes. This would be a letter, either from Rasia or from Lucien himself, and Isabella was not at all sure she wanted to read it. Finally, she resigned herself completely to it and picked it up off the floor. Unfolding it, she was relieved to see only Rasia's script across the page.

Dearest Isabella,

It is with great joy that I invite you to Lucien's sixteenth birthday! Finally, he reaches the goal that we have all been waiting so anxiously for!

With that being said, it is important to me that you understand how pained I have been to watch the events of the last three years unfold. I have been terribly aware of your pain, and while I cannot personally relate to it, I have felt it with you, to a certain extent. Please, Isabella, accept my apology, and the apology that I now extend to you on behalf of my son and the Family's future Master, Lucien.

While he does not yet offer this to you himself, he will. He is as aware of his destiny as you are of yours, more so now than ever. I am sure this is difficult for you to understand, so I ask you not only for your forgiveness but your continued grace and patience as well.

I am overjoyed at the prospect of seeing you here for dinner and the party on his birthday, June 6. The menu is designed with you in mind, dear. Know that I care deeply for you and your position, and hope you will respond with positive news that you will be attending.

Affectionately,

Rasia DeSai

Isabella reread the letter twice. Yes, she would attend, as would her parents. She would respond such in writing, as was proper. At least, when her own sixteenth birthday arrived in September, she could count on Lucien's presence this time.

She went to her desk and took out a sheet of her own flowered stationery, and she penned this response:

Dear Rasia and Lucien,

I am writing in response to the invitation you have extended my family and me to attend Lucien's long-awaited sixteenth birthday. All three of us are excited to celebrate with you both, and we will attend both the dinner and the party afterward.

Thank you for the invitation, and we will see you on June 6 at 7:00pm.

Cordially,

Isabella Gilliam and Family

She proofread the letter then folded it and placed it into a matching envelope, which she addressed without sealing. Mother would want to read it before it went out. She stood and headed back downstairs, where her mother was reading a newspaper in the living room.

"I have responded in writing to the invitation. I assume you will want to read it before you send it to the DeSais," she told her mother from the doorway.

Rose looked up and smiled. "Good girl," she said. "Let's see it."

Her mother took the envelope from her and removing the letter, scanned it with her eyes, not once, but twice. She then laid it on her lap and smiled at her daughter.

"I knew you would come around," she said quietly. "I appreciate the girl you are and the woman you are becoming, Isabella. Thank you."

Rose replaced the letter and sealed the envelope. "I will have daddy's assistant take it to the White House today. He is here meeting with him in the office."

Isabella nodded and turned and left the room in silence. It was the right thing to do, no matter how she felt about it. The smile of approval and the loving look her mother gave her was proof enough of that.

Isabella returned to her room to cry and say

goodbye to the life she had been planning. As of June 6th, it would be over for good, a part of her past, just as the last three years were quickly becoming. She hoped that soon she would feel emotionally safe enough to let her guard down for the sake of the family, and the destiny of her and Lucien DeSai.

∞

"Thank you for delivering this to me, Roger," Rasia said to Patrick's assistant. He had just handed her a flowered envelope with Isabella's writing on the front.

The man nodded and smiled. "Well, I need to get going, Queen. Patrick has prepared numerous tasks for me to complete in the next two days, and it is important that I get started."

"Of course. Take care now, and extend my gratitude to the Gilliams for me, will you?" With that Rasia closed the door softly and took the letter into the family room to read in private. She sat in her wing-backed chair and turned the envelope over in her hands. Isabella had always been such a good girl; it was a shame she had suffered for so long. Had Rasia had her way, she would have had a daughter, and the girl would have been just like Isabella Gilliam.

Rasia opened the envelope and removed the short note inside. She read it only once, and it made her smile. Isabella had written it while in pain, obviously, but she had not let her emotions dictate her words or her decision. Rasia would have expected no less from the extraordinary young woman.

She rose and went up the stairs, letter in hand, to

Lucien's room. She knocked lightly on the door.

"Lucien, I need to speak with you," she said through the door.

She heard him clear his throat, and in seconds the door opened. He stood there and said nothing, only looked at her expectantly, his eyes full of depression and pain. She held the letter up for him to see.

"I have already received a response from Isabella," she said with a smile.

Now she had his attention. "What did she say?" he asked his mother anxiously.

"She will be here, just as I knew she would," Rasia replied.

Lucien nodded, breathing out a heavy sigh of relief. "Thank you." He closed the door.

Rasia turned and walked away. He had been obviously relieved, for he knew that his behavior, no matter how out of his control, had hurt his lifelong friend and first lover. In his mind it was unforgivable, and she knew he had been very worried lately that no reconciliation would ever take place.

∞

Only two days ago, when she had sent out the invitation, they had discussed it fully.

"I think it is pointless to invite any of the Gilliams," Lucien had said. "Isabella is through with me."

Rasia had simply smiled and went about addressing the envelope. "You don't know that. I am beginning to wonder if you ever really knew her at all, or have you just forgotten?"

He had begun to pace back and forth in her office. "What will I do if she will not come? I will never find another like her, one that… knows me so well and accepts me."

"No, you are correct, you will not," she told him, looking up at him with stern eyes to drive her point home. "But you shouldn't fear. The Powers have chosen her, Lucien. They are in true control; not Isabella, not me, and not you."

She had left the room and taken the letter to Martin to be delivered to the Gilliams, leaving the boy alone in her office. The concern he felt was good for him; it would build character. Let him stew and learn from it.

Now she walked into her office and closed the door behind her. It was essential that she keep up her recordings in the Book. Someday Lucien would need all the information inside to guide him, both the witch and the vampire within his body. She retrieved the Book from the safe and opened it on her desk, where she began to write.

∞

"Lucien, you will begin a new phase of your learning today," Rasia said. Lucien had just come into the classroom, where his mother had been teaching him college courses for nearly two years.

He sat at his desk and looked at her. "What new phase?"

"Well, today we will take a trip to Cliffside Wineries, the pride of your father Cyril," she began. "You will begin to learn all of its workings and meet the people there. It will be your responsibility to keep it running and make sure things continue as he wished."

"So my destiny is to run a winery?" he asked her with sarcasm.

Rasia laughed out loud. "No, Lucien, but it is a part of it. Others will run it for you, but you are the ultimate overseer."

She watched his face; he calmed right down. "You will also begin to learn leadership on a very profound level. Your lessons will no longer consist of textbooks. You will learn how to properly govern and 'love' the Family."

He continued to look at her as he turned this new information over in his mind. Good, he decided. It was definitely a step in the right direction, the direction he wanted to go in. "Fine," he said. "When do these 'new lessons' begin?"

"This afternoon," she replied. "Effective immediately, morning classes will no longer be held. I will take the mornings and handle business, then after lunch, daily, we will either go to Cliffside or engage in other forms of teaching which are in keeping with your future. We will go to Cliffside today. Enjoy your morning." With a distracted wave of her hand, he was dismissed from her presence.

Lucien rose and left quickly. Cliffside Wineries indeed, he thought. He supposed it was only right. His mother had told him on several occasions about the love for wine both she and his father had, and she had also let him know that his father had been a master at making wines. Yes, he would do what was right, but only for the sake of his father.

Lucien often thought about his father, the stranger Cyril DeSai. He had seen photographs and videos. His mother had told him much about him, at least from what she knew. The knowledge that his mother had taken him from this Earth was what drove Lucien's murderous rage toward her. What would his life have been like had Cyril been in it? Certainly, he would have been more prepared for his heritage than Rasia had made him.

He went outside and walked in the courtyard, enjoying the morning air that he so rarely got to breathe. He continued to think about Cyril and Rasia, and the more he pondered, the angrier he got toward that woman who called herself his mother. Oh, her end was coming soon.

He had plotted and schemed more furiously than ever lately, and on two recent occasions, he had stooped to silly means in an effort to eliminate her from the face of the Earth. Four months ago, he had introduced cyanide into a glass of Shiraz she had him pour for her; it had absolutely no effect, and the dose had been substantial. All that had happened was Rasia had become tired more quickly than usual and retired early for the night. When Lucien woke to find her at the breakfast table the next morning, he had been furious, and he was forced to continue to bide his time and plan her death.

Then, only a month ago, he had snuck into her

room while she was sleeping. He had worked up his courage and taken a huge risk: he injected her with a massive amount of tranquilizer while she slept. She hadn't stirred, not even when he pricked her thigh with the needle. The next morning she appeared at the breakfast table as if nothing had happened yet again. Lucien ended up checking the expiration dates on the vials of drugs and found they had lost their potency at least two years ago. He threw them, and the accompanying syringes, in the incinerator.

After those two incidents, he had come to a standstill. She was, indeed, a vampire, and short of doing to her what she had done to his father he had no idea what would work. All Lucien knew was that he wanted her dead. He often had to remind himself that his day with her would come, one way or another, and all he had to do was be patient.

He would have to come up with another way.

He had finally reached the solid conclusion that when the perfect opportunity arose, he would take off her head, just as she had done to Cyril. He would be sure he had the strength first, of course, and that would not be until he was sixteen, or shortly thereafter. It wouldn't do to have her knock him across the room as she had done when he tried to attack her at thirteen. No, he must make sure he was stronger than she, and the good news was that this was right around the corner.

He would indulge her demands and wishes until then. But Lucien knew that soon, very soon, Rasia

DeSai would know how his father had felt the night she ripped his head from his body. He would pay her back for her sin, and he would wipe her out completely.

Lucien smiled and began to hum as he strolled.

R.W.K. Clark

CHAPTER 17

The limousine glided along the highway as if it were on rails. Rasia and Lucien sat in the back enjoying the relaxing ride, both of them sipping cold lemonade. They were on their way to Cliffside together for the first time in Lucien's life, and although his initial reaction to her news of their trip that morning had been less than favorable, he found himself feeling a bit of excitement at seeing his father's place of business.

Rasia had hoped that the two of them would chat on the drive. In the last two years, her son's scent had ceased to bother her, and she had attempted to reach out to him on numerous occasions. He was always far less than receptive, though, and this trip proved no different. She made a couple of attempts to engage him in conversation, but both times he responded to her efforts with single-word replies. She had finally given up, and their ride had continued in silence.

Lucien enjoyed the scenery, and the trip made him realize how much of the world he had never seen or experienced. Rasia had educated him fully on geography; he was aware of how large the planet was and all it held. Now, as he stared at the rolling, grassy hills, his hatred toward her grew even more. Look at all he had missed!

He was still staring out his window when his mother said, "Look, Lucien, there it is!"

Lucien shifted his gaze to the windshield and saw the massive stone structure. It was more a mansion than a place of business, but he should have expected that. It had been a private residence centuries ago. He could just see what he assumed were the vineyards off in the distance, and there were several other buildings which surrounded the main offices. He also took note of the parking lot, which was filled with vehicles.

Their driver took the long, narrow road that led to the main entrance, then pulled the car up to the double doors, which were situated under a great burgundy-colored awning. Lucien took note that the awning looked brand new, with no signs of weathering or wear.

"Well, here we are," Rasia said with a smile as the limo came to a full stop. She turned to Lucien. "Are you nervous?"

"Of course not," he replied.

"Well, good," she said. "Then you will find this enjoyable, I believe. You will love your father's taste in art and sculpture."

They got out of the car and Lucien came around to his mother's side, where he stood looking all around him, taking in as much detail as he could. It was certainly a beautiful place, he had to admit. He wondered what the people were like. Would any of them had known his father?

Rasia took him by the arm and began to lead him up the steps of the main entrance. "When Cyril stepped into the United States presidency, he took up residence at the White House. Until then, he resided full time right here," she began.

The chauffeur opened the main entrance door for them, bowing slightly as they walked through the threshold. The door closed with a muted 'swoosh' behind them. Lucien's mouth fell open as he looked around at the foyer; it was simply spectacular.

The paintings and sculptures were all dark in nature but breathtaking in execution. Everything was done in red and black, and it suited the spirit of the place perfectly. He walked up to a gargoyle with long teeth perched on a pedestal; he would swear that the eyes of the statue were alive. He could not resist stroking the cold stone that made up its body. Poor, poor baby, he thought.

A strange female voice broke through into his thoughts. "Queen! It is wonderful to see you once again, and you have brought Lucien, our Master!"

"Yes, Shirley. Lucien, this is Shirley Louis. She is the executive assistant to main management, Martin Steenway. She was also your father's personal assistant before he moved to Washington," said Rasia.

Lucien turned to the woman and smiled. She was attractive, in a dumpy sort of way, but he could see the great admiration in her eyes. She obviously cared about his father very, very much. He extended his hand to her, smiling.

"Hello, Shirley, I am Lucien," he said.

The woman blushed a deep red and took his hand, bowing. "Oh, Master, there is no mistaking that! You are the spitting image of your father."

This statement pleased Lucien to no end. It made him sick to think he may resemble Rasia in any way. He squeezed the woman's hand warmly, then raised it to his lips and kissed it gently.

"You don't know how much that means to me," he said. "Thank you."

Shirley blushed again. "And you behave like him as well."

The woman was older, though she looked to be in her twenties. That was the best part of being a vampire, Lucien knew. Eternal youth. But even though she was attractive enough, he felt no desire whatsoever; as a matter of fact, seducing her didn't even cross his mind.

Rasia interrupted the woman's worshipful trance. "Shirley, beginning today Lucien will begin to learn about the winery. Today he will tour, meet the staff, and have his dinner here."

"Would you like me to call a guide to accompany you?" Shirley asked.

Rasia shook her head. "No," she replied. "I will do the honors myself, thank you."

With that, Shirley Louis bowed slightly, first to Rasia then to Lucien, and then walked away. Rasia turned to her son and smiled again.

"Are you ready? I thought I would show you around first. You can meet people as we encounter them, yes?"

Lucien nodded, feeling truly eager for the very first time. "Yes."

The two walked into the main reception area. There was the main desk with a very young auburn-haired woman seated behind it. Others were milling around, but as soon as everyone became aware of Lucien and Rasia's presence, all activity ceased.

"Good afternoon, everyone," Rasia began. She took Lucien by the arm once again, and though he cringed inside, he allowed her the luxury. "This is Lucien, the son of Cyril and I. He will be touring the facilities today."

Gasps could be heard all around, then smiles broke out. His mother introduced him to all present, and each bowed down to him and kissed his hand when he offered it for shaking. Lucien found himself overwhelmed with the worshipful attention. It was beginning to sink in; he was, indeed, someone quite special.

First, he and Rasia visited every office and room from the ground floor up. Lucien met everyone they came into contact with, and the reception they gave him was always the same. He met Martin Steenway, who proved to be nothing more than an attentive brown-noser, but what could be expected? Perhaps the man thought that Lucien intended to remove him from his position, but he had nothing to worry about.

Next Rasia took him to the other buildings on the property. In brief, she explained the function and purpose of every single one, even taking him to the vineyards and the stables. He loved the carriages and made a mental note that he and Isabella would visit here and take a ride.

Lucien found he was completely taken with the entire winemaking process. Everyone he met at each station would explain how things worked, and Lucien soaked up all the information like a sponge. He asked intelligent questions, and his mother even allowed him to sample one red wine and one white. She loved wine, and could not wait to share it with him, he could tell.

He found he had a taste for it as well, which only proved to stoke his interest in Cliffside. Yes, he would rule the world, but he would pay special attention to this little corner of it. He was excited, and he found he could hardly wait for the future.

When he and Rasia were done touring the grounds, they returned to the main building, where they took a private room off the cafeteria. A rich dinner of escargot in wine sauce was served with wild rice and fresh green beans. For dessert, they enjoyed a wonderful bread pudding, and Rasia allowed him to choose a glass of wine on his own to enjoy with his dinner.

It was, quite possibly, the only enjoyable day he had with his mother in his life.

When they were leaving the cafeteria, Rasia stopped and turned to him. "Now I want you to see your father's quarters."

"His office?" Lucien asked. "Who uses it now?"

Rasia began walking again. "No one," she replied. "Well, I do, when I need it. But it remains his and his alone."

They grabbed the elevator at the far end of the hall and Rasia pushed the very last button. It was inscribed with the initials 'CD', which were done in fine script on the button. The elevator slowly began to move, and the two rode down in silence.

When the doors opened, Lucien sucked in his breath. He slowly stepped out, overwhelmed by the sight before him. There was a long hall, dark and powerful. There were exquisite statues on rows of pedestals on both sides of the hall, all the way to the end. There were no man-made lights, only candles, which proved to be more than sufficient.

Lucien walked slowly toward the massive black double doors at the end, stopping to view and caress each and every sculpture on his way. At the very last one, he took notice of the walls. The figures and images on it were alive and moving, living out violent yet beautiful scenes depicting lust and murder. It appeared and smelled as if these images were in blood.

The blood of those who are no longer living, he thought. This is perfect.

He stopped at the doors and turned. Rasia still remained next to the elevator. "What do you think so far?" she asked him.

Lucien sucked in his breath. "It is magnificent."

"Yes, dear," she replied softly. "I know."

She approached him, sorting through a ring of keys in her hand. When she got to the doors, she inserted a large black skeleton key set with a ruby into the single lock on the door on the right. It swung open slowly, showing only darkness, but as the two entered the room, candles on the walls began to light, one by one.

Once again, Rasia remained by the door and allowed Lucien to freely roam. After all, this would be his; she had no right to stop him. He advanced slowly, beginning on his left, then working his way slowly in a circle around the room. He did not want to miss anything.

The office had the same incredible walls as the hall, but the sculptures inside were much more detailed and intense. Each and every statue had a face and eyes that were alive and knowing, and each depicted a scene of passion mixed with pain. He was completely enraptured by them all.

The fireplace was massive and black, like everything else. It had lit when they entered, allowing him to see the pair of chaise lounges before it, and the blood-red carpet that covered the floor beneath them. There was no dust, no dirt. Everything sparkled and shone, and he found he was very pleased with that fact.

Finally, he came to his father's desk. It was like everything else, but when Lucien stood before it, his father's presence became tangible to him. He looked at the pens and papers which sat quietly on top, and he could almost see Cyril DeSai sitting in the leather chair behind it.

He placed both of his hands palms-down on the surface of the desk. Suddenly, he was filled with a warmth that was tinged with ice, and it crept through every vein in his body, coursing through him like blood. Then Lucien had a vision.

It was his mother and father. They were seated by the fire, his mother on one of the lounges, and his father on its edge. Cyril's eyes were filled with love as he gazed at Rasia and spoke to her about his life. Lucien could hear the entire conversation between them, and he paid close attention to their words.

Then the two were making love. Lucien felt no shame or embarrassment at what he was seeing, even though he knew the sight to be the truth. He knew this had been their first time together, and he was aware fully that it would be their last. His father was showing it all to him.

He continued to stare at the desk, his vision obscured by the images in his mind's eye. Now they were finished, and the look on his father's face had changed from one of intense love to one of dire concern. Suddenly, Rasia took his father by the hair and ripped his head violently from his body. The vision left him.

Lucien gasped aloud and jerked his head up. He turned to Rasia; she looked as though she had no idea of what he had just gone through.

"Do you like it, Lucien?" she asked simply. "It is to be yours. I hope it suits you."

He held her gaze. "Yes, it will do," he replied in a low voice.

She was nothing more than a selfish murderess who deserved everything she got. He found he was more than happy to be the one to give it to her. How he could hardly contain himself at the thought of revenge! She had stolen his father, and he would take her life someday very, very soon.

Lucien straightened his face and muffled the fury within him. "It is actually perfect, Mother," he continued, his voice lightening. Rasia knit her brow; his disposition had just shifted drastically, from good to bad, then to good once again. She felt uncomfortable but pushed it aside.

"You are free to make any changes you like when you take over, but I think it is perfect here," she stated lightly.

He looked around one final time and took a deep breath. "No," he told her. "No changes will be necessary. I couldn't imagine a better sanctuary of peace than this."

With that Lucien turned to her abruptly. "I am quite tired now, surprisingly. Are you ready to head home?"

Rasia searched his face and nodded slowly. "Yes," she said. "Let's go. We will return often enough in the near future."

Together the two of them left the office, which Rasia locked up tightly. They took the elevator back to the main floor, and soon enough they had bid farewell to the staff on site. In no time they were back in the limo, heading for Washington, DC and the White House.

The drive home was silent. Rasia did not press him for opinions or thoughts. She assumed the sight of

Cliffside, especially his father's former office, had affected Lucien in a powerful way. She wanted to let him be with his own mind.

Lucien, on the other hand, was not thinking of Cliffside at all. He was pondering his mother's death. He was daydreaming of her blood running through his hands.

R.W.K. Clark

CHAPTER 18

Rose and Isabella sat at the breakfast nook in their kitchen. They had just had breakfast and were now chatting about Isabella's current college lessons. It had been six weeks since they had received the invitation to Lucien's birthday, and Isabella had come around exceptionally well.

After a short silence, Rose spoke. "Lucien has been learning about the workings at Cliffside Wineries. He has toured it, and Martin Steenway, the man who runs it, has been teaching him the ropes."

Isabella continued to gaze out the window. "So, he will take over operations there?"

"Yes and no," Rose replied. "His primary responsibility will be to the Family, but the winery will be his. It is important that he learn it. According to Rasia, he has taken to it like a fish to water. It seems he is a natural winemaker."

Isabella nodded but showed no real enthusiasm. In reality, she was very happy. It sounded like he was becoming a man after all. Maybe she shouldn't be so apprehensive about their pending reconciliation.

"He is also taking some intense lessons on

leadership. I saw him with Rasia the other day, and I think he has grown in leaps and bounds, Isabella," her mother said.

Finally, the girl turned to Rose. "I have to be honest, Mother. I am very happy that Lucien is turning out to be everything we all hoped," she said. "But please keep in mind that I must grieve all that I am going to lose in my compliance." She stood and straightened her shirt nervously. "You will have to let me do that in my own time."

Rose nodded. "I understand, dear. I only thought that good news would move the process along." The last thing she ever wanted to do was hurt the heart of her beloved daughter, and every thought or action that Rose had in this life was designed for Isabella's good. She had to remember that her daughter was nearly a full-grown woman, and she would have to find her way on many issues on her own.

Isabella squeezed her mother's shoulder affectionately and then left the room. Yes, good news about Lucien helped, but it did nothing to diminish the resentment she felt. She could admit that it was lessening, but she refused to be rushed.

In a month and a half, her life would change drastically yet again. She would step into her destiny willingly, but at this point in time, she no longer felt the love for Lucien she once felt. No, she felt the obligation. Maybe in time, her love could be rekindled, but for now…

Lucien was, indeed, a natural when it came to making wine. He began to spend as much of his free time as he could at the facilities, and his mother allowed him free use of the limo for that purpose. When he was home, he studied winemaking, and he even studied his father's ancient notes and records on the craft. Over the course of the few months leading up to his sixteenth birthday, Lucien not only introduced new wines and improved on existing labels. But he also showed a great capacity for the business aspect of Cliffside, and Rasia could not have been happier.

For leadership, she engaged him in outside activities that included the Family. Once she had him prepare a speech on loyalty and respect, then she had him present it to members of the Family in a small town in Massachusetts. The people there had been having intense and violent disagreements, and on a couple of occasions, Family members had murdered each other for simple reasons.

His speech was intended to give the people hope for their eternal future on Earth, the future the Powers had given to them all. He would be leading them after two years, and they needed to know he had their best interests at heart. Not only did he succeed in reassuring them of this, but he also left their presence with a sure knowledge that things would settle down there. He had made them all well aware that consequences for antagonistic behavior amongst his people would be inevitable if it continued, but he also assured them of his love and concern for them all.

The funny thing to Lucien was that he was beginning to feel a powerful affection for others in the Family. Everyone but Rasia that is. Her presence and her very scent made the rage inside of him boil. He was thankful to the Powers that he was able to contain himself until her time was due.

∞

Now Lucien's sixteenth birthday was one week away. Yes, it would mean full manhood for him, but he would not come fully into his true power and destiny until he was eighteen. In the meantime, he would learn all he could.

The overwhelming desire for sex which he had experienced for the last three years had all but disappeared. He still craved it, and now and then he indulged himself, but not often. All he could think about was Isabella now. He was anxious to have her once again. He knew deep inside that he would not know sexual fulfillment apart from her. Most of all, he couldn't wait to favor her with all he had learned. He only hoped she would have him back.

Only one week, Lucien thought to himself. One week and I will see Isabella. Soon after that, I will rid the world of Rasia the parasite once and for all.

∞

Isabella stood in her room with a red silk jersey dress on. Her mother was pinning it here and there. They were making the dress together, and it was turning out to be amazing. It would fit her figure perfectly, and it would be striking when it was complete. Just a few adjustments and some black lace embellishments and she would have the perfect dress to wear to Lucien's party.

She wanted Lucien to see what he had been missing. At nearly sixteen, Isabella was indeed a grown woman physically. Her breasts were full and firm, her waist small, and her hips perfectly formed. Her flat stomach topped her figure off perfectly. Her long blond hair fell all the way past her waist in great curls, and her eyes were so blue they hypnotized any male she talked to. She was unspeakably beautiful.

Now she was mentally preparing herself to see her first love once again. It was fast approaching, and she found she was more excited and nervous than resentful. The negative feelings were dissipating as the date grew near, and she was glad, but for the time being, she fully intended to make him squirm. Yes, he would want her again, but she would see to it that he only wanted her and her alone.

Rose carefully helped her remove the dress so the final adjustments could be made. Isabella took her box of jewelry and sat on her bed. She removed a ruby and onyx pendant which hung on a thin gold chain. She also chose the earrings that matched it. She would wear a single ruby solitaire on her right hand, and a gold chain bracelet on her left wrist.

Yes, she would be stunning. It seemed she could barely contain herself as she planned in her head. Soon she would see Lucien. Was he bigger, more mature in behavior? What would he be like now, three years later?

Isabella smiled and daydreamed as she hummed to herself, and beside her Rose smiled, satisfied that things were finally going to work out for them all.

CHAPTER 19

Lucien stood before the full-length mirror in his personal bathroom. He had just showered and dressed, and he was making sure he looked as good as he felt. Today was his sixteenth birthday, a day he had long waited for; nothing else would do.

He wore black tailored trousers, a black formal button-down shirt, and a black silk dinner jacket with tails. His tie was long and narrow, and it was blood-red in color, as were the cuffs of his button-down, and the lapels of his jacket. He wore black wing-tip Italian leather shoes, and his blood-red socks were silk also.

On his left pinkie finger, Lucien wore a ruby stone, and his cufflinks and tie-tack were 18-karat gold. His goatee was combed into an immaculate point at his chin, and his long, jet-black hair was pulled back into a ponytail which hung down his back in a thick rope. Yes, he thought to himself, this will do.

Tonight he would see Isabella for the first time since that disaster at the Festival. Even though the memory was little more than a blur in his mind, he still could recall the sickness he felt in his stomach when she saw him with that worthless excuse for a piece of ass. How humiliating! How would she ever really forgive him? She had seen him with a girl who was no more than Family trash, a slave to the grind. Compared to Isabella, she was no more than a sea slug, and the wretched memory of the confrontation was shameful and sickening.

He took one final look at his reflection then left the bathroom. It was now six-thirty; the Gilliams would be here directly at seven. Isabella's parents did not believe in being late, or early for that matter. Lucien took a deep breath; tonight was the night.

He made his way down the stairs slowly. He was determined to carry himself with dignity and grace. He would display nothing but strength and respect because he knew Isabella. She would not accept anything less, not if she were still his Isabella. But what if she were not? The thought was more distressing than anything he had considered in his life. What if his deviant behavior had killed the gorgeous, gentle Isabella he once had?

Mother was in the family room, and the servants were still preparing the dining area for dinner. He entered the room with full confidence. The nasty woman loved to criticize him, but he dared her to find anything wrong with him tonight. He was ideal in appearance and carriage.

Rasia was dressed in green silk, and her make-up was perfect. She had pulled her hair up into a curly bun on top of her head, with ringlets hanging around her face. Emeralds graced her ears, neck, and fingers. Green always had brought out her eyes, Lucien thought. Her eyes were the most attractive part of the woman herself.

Once she was dead, he would miss her green eyes most of all.

She looked up at her son, and her eyes lit brightly. Rasia stood immediately, dropping the book she had been reading to the floor without a thought.

"Lucien, you are stunning," Rasia told him, her voice gushing. "Isabella will never be able to deny you."

"Thank you, Mother," he replied, standing straight before her. "I am nervous nonetheless."

Rasia bent down to retrieve her reading, her smile plastered to her face. "Now, that's to be expected," she told him. "Just remember, it is meant to be."

For the next little, while the two conversed in small talk, and Martin Lamb joined them after a bit. He looked the same as he looked daily, sporting a regular business suit and striped tie. Ever the politician was Martin Lamb, even in the blessed absence of all politics.

Lucien's stomach began to churn, and he felt a slight sense of vertigo for a brief moment. Right then the doorbell chimed, and all three of them looked at each other. The guests had arrived.

Rasia finally spoke. "Well, it's not going to do for us to sit here and look at each other," she said. She brushed past both Lucien and Martin to let the Gilliams in. Lucien looked at Martin, who had nothing to offer the young man but a sheepish smile.

"You're on, Lucien," he said.

The two men arrived at the front door as Rasia was gushing over Rose's dress. At first, Lucien saw only Patrick and his wife. Where was Isabella? Suddenly, the girl appeared behind her father and stepped into the door.

Lucien lost his breath. Was this his Isabella, the girl he had always known? Certainly not! This was a full-grown woman, and she was the most exquisite creature he had ever seen. The scent of her body filled his nostrils immediately, though, and he knew that it was she.

"Isabella," Rasia began, "the Powers have certainly been good to you! You are striking!" She embraced the girl fully, beaming with the pleasure of seeing her once again after such a long time.

Isabella smiled shyly at Rasia. "Thank you," she said softly before taking her father's arm. Rasia hurried to shut the door behind them.

While Martin and their three guests busied themselves with greetings, Lucien stood frozen. He could not take his eyes off of Isabella. Why did she take no notice of him? Why did she not even glance his way?

He knew that he would have to take the upper hand, he would have to break the ice. He breathed in deeply and then advanced slowly, making his way to the angel before him. He could only hope his advances in conversing would go smoothly, even though he wanted to throw up.

"Hello, Isabella," he said, touching her arm softly. "It has certainly been too long."

Finally, she turned to him and looked at him. "You are looking well, Lucien. Happy birthday."

He opened his mouth to speak, but nothing came

out. Lucien finally cleared his throat. "Thank you. Would you like to come into the family room? We are having drinks in there."

Isabella looked to Patrick, who nodded at her and smiled. "Sure, I suppose so," she said. Lucien offered her his arm, but she hesitated. Finally, she took it, and the two of them went into the family room, with the others right behind them.

"What would you like to drink, Isabella?" Lucien asked her.

She glanced back at her parents. "My parents said I can only have wine tonight."

Lucien smiled. "Red or white?"

"I would like Chardonnay, please," Isabella said.

This pleased the young man. As he prepared her wine, he told her, "This is one of ours, and it happens to be one I made changes of improvement too. Tell me how you like it."

He handed her the glass, and as she took it, her fingers brushed his. Electricity shot up his arm, and he caught his breath. Oh, where had she come from, this satin angel of light?

Isabella lifted the glass slowly to her lips and sipped at the chilled wine. She closed her eyes. "It is delicious."

"Have you had the opportunity to indulge before tonight?" he asked her.

She opened her eyes and nodded, swirling the wine in her glass. "Yes, mother and I enjoy it together. I have tasted many."

"Let's sit," Lucien suggested.

The two had a seat on a velvet loveseat under a bay window. Isabella was nervous, but Lucien could not tell. This was a very composed and poised young woman, and he wanted to have her then and there. He had not felt such desire in months, and he could almost taste her scent in his mouth.

"I hardly recognized you, Isabella. You are so beautiful," he began.

She took another sip of her wine, then said, "Thank you."

"Look at me, please," Lucien asked, his voice low but urgent.

Isabella met his gaze. The two looked at each other for a long moment before Lucien finally spoke. "I am so very, very sorry," he whispered.

"Me too," Isabella whispered back.

They sat in silence for a long time, sipping their wines and letting the air settle around them. He had apologized, and Isabella knew that was all he could do; the ball was now in her court, and she had to manage it in a manner conducive to the proper and expected end result.

In true Isabella-fashion, she pushed her emotions to the bottom of her stomach. "Mother said you have been preparing to run Cliffside, and for your reign."

Lucien glanced in the direction of the adults. They all stood together, cackling and gabbing. He looked back at Isabella. "Yes, and I love it. I am more than ready, I believe."

She looked him over, then looked back at her wine

glass. "You very well may be," she said. "Time will tell."

One of the servants, an older gray-haired woman, appeared at the door. "Dinner is served when you all are ready."

Rasia turned to Lucien and Isabella. "Bring your glasses and come enjoy. Isabella, Lucien and I chose this meal with you in mind, you know."

"Thank you," she replied. "I have been looking forward to it."

She stood, and Lucien stood with her. He took her gently by the arm and allowed her to leave before him. The smell of her was like a drug which he could not get enough of. It was soft and sweet, like the aroma of flowers, yet it was musky and womanly, which he did not recall detecting before when they had been together. The mix had him reeling.

Dinner was wonderful. Rare leg of lamb, roasted baby potatoes with herbs, and parmesan asparagus. The wine was flowing, and so was the conversation. Lucien sat at one end of the table, and Isabella was strategically seated next to him. He took advantage of her presence by telling her all about the winery and the speeches he had been giving. Then he asked her about her own life.

"So, what have you been doing?" he asked, much more relaxed now. "I am dying to hear."

Isabella swallowed her food and took a drink of her wine. "I completed regular studies nearly two years ago, and since then I have studied all forms of history with students from the university."

"You have attended the University?" This got his

attention. Had she been with other boys or men? Did she date? Maybe she even had another boyfriend entirely! He was nearly sick with panic, but he managed it, keeping himself fully composed.

Isabella nodded. "Yes, but not physically," she replied. "I attend digitally, over the television."

It was all he could do to keep from breathing a sigh of relief, but he still had to know. "Have you seen anyone?"

Isabella's eyes flashed fire. "Would it matter if I had?" Her voice was as sharp as a knife, and even Lucien flinched.

"No, I suppose it wouldn't now, would it?" She was right; he had no business questioning her at all.

The girl calmed herself. "Since you mentioned it, no, I have never dated. It was not a luxury a girl in my position was afforded."

She turned her attention back to her plate, signifying that she was done with this particular topic. Lucien did the same, embarrassed that he had been so bold. He had done nothing but put this girl through some kind of personal hell for three years, he could see it in her eyes. The same eyes that used to caress him now stabbed at him.

This was all Rasia's fault. If she had been honest from the beginning, he could have been better prepared for his life. If she had left his father living, his father would have taught him, and things would have gone much more smoothly. Oh, how he wanted her dead! He looked at her down the length of the table, laughing at some joke Martin had told. Her day would come.

The servants appeared with the birthday cake: rich chocolate with a thick raspberry glaze, another of Isabella's favorites. Lucien saw her eyes light up at the sight of it, and for a brief second, he saw the girl inside of the woman. It made him ache inside.

After the candles were blown out and the songs were sung, all of them enjoyed the rich dessert before them. A conversation between the two began once again, but this time they discussed maybe spending a bit more time together.

"I would like to visit with you sometime again, another day," Lucien began. "I hope you will find it in your heart to forgive me."

Isabella rubbed her full stomach. "I forgive you, Lucien, I just need more time."

"Good," he replied. "Time is something we always have."

Suddenly Rasia stood. "There are gifts in the recreation room, and we can have more cocktails there. Let's go!"

With that, the group made their way out of the dining room to watch Lucien open his gifts.

R.W.K. Clark

CHAPTER 20

Lucien found himself showered with gifts that night, including his very first automobile, a brand new black Jaguar F Type. While he was pleased with all he received, the presence of Isabella kept him distracted. All he could think about was being alone with her.

The group laughed and enjoyed each other's company until just after eleven, at which point Lucien had worked up enough courage to try and get Isabella alone. He was thinking steadily about having sex with her, but he knew his Isabella; this would not be something that would take place right away. He realized that if he wanted to get close to her again, he would have to bide his time.

He noticed Rose yawning, and knew they would be leaving soon. He turned to Isabella. "Would you consider a short walk in the courtyard with me before you go?"

She looked down at her hands, thinking how to respond. He watched her closely. She was so wonderful! She was wearing a red silk dress that hugged her curves, and it had black lace around the neckline. He had only realized just that moment that the colors they wore were the same, and he knew they must have looked perfect together.

Finally, she looked up at him. "Sure, Lucien, but there will be nothing happening. Not even a kiss."

He simply nodded and took her by the hand. They stood, and he turned to the others. "Isabella and I are going to visit the courtyard for a few minutes. I hope you all don't mind."

"Of course not," Rasia said, smiling. "Take a bit of time to visit alone before the Gilliams leave. Are you okay with that, Isabella?"

The girl smiled. "Yes, thank you."

With that, he led her from the room, his hand gently on her arm. They did not speak until they were in the courtyard alone. Lucien started the conversation.

"The party was nice," he began. "My mother seems pleased."

Isabella laughed lightly. "Yes, but she is one determined for things to be perfect."

"I know," he replied. "It is a beautiful night."

A breeze caught Isabella's hair, and Lucien could not take his eyes off of her. "You look more astonishing than ever. I just want you to know that I see it."

"Lucien, you have a way to go to gain my trust," she said.

He nodded. "I realize this, but it cannot be done without time spent together."

"I know," she replied. "Just keep in mind that it will be slow going for a while. I am not in a hurry to have my heart broken."

Lucien gently squeezed her hand. "I will never be the one to break your heart again. Isabella, try to understand that I… I seemed to be out of my own mind, even to me."

"I cannot understand it," she said. "It has been explained to me, but as a woman, it is not something I am capable of grasping."

Once again he nodded. "I don't suppose so. I don't understand it myself."

They walked in silence for a while, just enjoying the night and the pleasure of being together once again. Lucien had so much he wanted to say, but he could not settle on any one thing. Finally, Isabella broke the silence.

"My parents will be ready to leave soon, Lucien," she began. "If you want me in your future, this is what I require of you."

"Tell me, Isabella. Anything," he replied.

She looked deep into his eyes. "We need to spend as much time together as possible. We are both busy so we will have to work it out."

Lucien smiled. "Go on."

"We will not have sex until your birthday next year," she stated boldly. "I need to know it is me and only me, and I need you to show me. You will remain faithful to me until your next birthday, and if you succeed, well, you shall have me as your seventeenth birthday gift."

Lucien's heart sank as quickly as it had soared. "What if I cannot?"

"Then you will not have me," she told him firmly.

He thought for only a moment before making his promise. "I understand, and I agree."

"Then I too am willing to put forth the needed effort." She turned and began to walk in the direction of the house. Lucien followed her like a puppy.

"When shall we get together next, Isabella?" He asked her eagerly.

She stopped and turned to him. "Do you have anything in mind?"

"How about Saturday? We could have lunch in town and maybe visit the Smithsonian together, would you like that?" he asked.

Isabella was pleased. He had done his homework regarding her recent interests. "I think it sounds wonderful. When and where should I meet you?"

"I would be honored to pick you up in my new car," he replied.

Isabella laughed loudly now. "Cool. When did you learn to drive anyway?"

It was Lucien's turn to laugh now; she almost sounded like her old self. "Martin has taught me. It made him a nervous wreck, but I am a fast learner."

"Oh, gosh," she said, rolling her eyes. "I can just imagine Martin Lamb in the passenger seat while you drive. What a riot it must have been!"

"It was entertaining to me, to say the least," he replied, and they laughed a bit more. "I will pick you up at your home Saturday at eleven-thirty, agreed?"

"I look forward to it, Lucien."

They returned to the house, where the Gilliams were

just arriving at the door to the courtyard to fetch their daughter. Isabella turned to Lucien once again. "Saturday at eleven-thirty then."

"Yes," he said.

She put her hand gently on his arm and leaned toward him slowly. Then Isabella quickly and lightly kissed him on the cheek. "Goodbye, for now, Lucien."

"Goodbye for now," Lucien replied, and then she was gone.

His hand went to his cheek, where her kiss still burned his flesh. How soft and delicate it had been, as the momentary landing of a butterfly. But like a butterfly, she had eluded him. He sighed and smiled. Yes, Isabella was his destiny.

Suddenly, he became aware of Rasia standing at the doorway to the family room. "Did it go well, Lucien?"

He dropped his hand self-consciously from his face; his mother's presence caught him off guard. "Yes, it went better than I expected," he said. "We will meet on Saturday, and we will begin to spend more time together. I must rebuild her trust in me."

"She said that?" Rasia asked. "That is rather wise of the girl, I believe, even though the outcome is inevitable."

"Yes, and she will not submit to me until my seventeenth birthday," he said, his voice low.

Now Rasia smiled. "Well, bide your time. It will likely happen sooner than that, but even if it doesn't, can you blame her?"

"No."

"If I were you, I would be on my best behavior," she continued. "I would not put it past Isabella to defy her own destiny for the sake of something as basic as trust, do you?"

"No, I do not," he said.

She nodded. "I am very tired Lucien. Tomorrow you visit Abingdon, Virginia and the Family there. I suggest you rest up. You will be flying, and Martin will accompany you. Have a good night." With that, she strode off toward her room.

Lucien did not wait long to follow. He wanted to spend a bit of time pondering the wonder that was Isabella. He still could not get her off his mind, and he expected he wouldn't be able to for a long time to come.

He changed his clothes and climbed in bed. As soon as his head touched the pillow, he was overcome with sleep. His last conscious thought was that of the way her skin felt, and the way her hair smelled. This was what love must feel like, he thought.

Isabella rode in the backseat of the family sedan, watching the distant lights of the city as she and her parents made the way home from Lucien's birthday celebration. At first the trio was quiet, but finally Rose could take no more. She turned toward her daughter in the back seat.

"Ok, spit it out," she said eagerly, a broad smile on her face. "What happened outside? Tell me all about it!"

Isabella smiled back. "Wow, Mom," she said, shaking her head. "You don't give a girl a minute to tease you, do you?"

"Not in this case."

"Well, we walked, and then Lucien started to be apologetic once again. He wants to get close again, but I told him it was going to take time for me to trust him."

Rose nodded. "What did he say?"

"He said he understood, and we agreed to start spending more time together. We have plans to meet for lunch on Saturday, and we are going to visit the Smithsonian together."

"Wow," her mother said with excitement. "A real date, and the first one at that!"

"Yes, a real date," Isabella replied. "But that's not all."

Now her father looked at her in the rearview mirror. "What do you mean?"

Isabella met his gaze in the mirror. "I told him I want one full year of faithfulness before I even begin to consider going any further," she said simply.

Both of her parents got a stricken look on their faces. "How did he respond to that?" Patrick asked with concern.

"Well, he voiced that he was not sure he could do it, as if he doesn't trust himself fully, either."

Patrick looked at the road. "He probably doesn't. It wasn't him, Isabella."

"I know that Daddy, but it is him now, and he is aware of what he had done," she stated firmly. "I need this. If it happens sooner, it happens. If not, well, we all shall see, now, won't we?"

Rose turned to face forward, and Patrick refocused on his driving. Isabella looked back out the window, but her father glanced at her now and again in the mirror. She was a smart one, his daughter, and she knew she deserved better than to be treated like a second choice. He would support her demands and help her be true to her heart. He loved her, and so did Rose.

They rode the rest of the way home in silence, but the atmosphere in the car was light. They all knew that they had crossed a milestone in the lives of Lucien and Isabella tonight, and that was vitally important. Satisfied, they all decided to enjoy the ride and go with the flow; the Powers would work it all out.

CHAPTER 21

Isabella stood at the front window in the family living room. She was a bit nervous and jittery. Lucien would arrive to pick her up for their lunch date any time now. She hoped it went okay; she so badly wanted everything to work out.

She chose simple, casual clothes for their first date: a pair of low-cut skinny jeans, a pair of red flats, and a red gauzy long-sleeved poet's shirt tucked in and set off with a red belt. She wore simple eyeliner and mascara, with rich red lipstick, and her hair hung loosely down her back. She hoped he approved.

She began to pace back and forth a bit. It was only ten minutes after eleven, but she wanted the initial ice-breaking to get here and pass. Her parents would invite him in for a moment, and she even had it on good authority that her father intended to talk privately to Lucien. She would let him have his 'man talk'; as a father, she was sure he needed it.

By a quarter after the hour, she had enough pacing and decided to change purses to pass the time. She jogged upstairs to her room and chose a black leather shoulder bag, then sat down on the bed to clean it out and switch the contents of her current purse into it.

She reached inside the bag and found a gum wrapper, an ink pen, and a smashed mini candy bar; the find made her smile. Then she reached into the outside zipper pocket and felt a piece of paper. She pulled it out and unfolded it. It was a note from Lucien, and it had to be five years old. Her mother had given her this purse for play when she was nine, so she guessed that to be about right.

The note had a very detailed drawing of the two of them holding hands. Behind them were several trees, and at the base of the trees, lay a person with his eyes and mouth covered; his hands were tied. A heart was drawn around the entire scene, and in ten-year-old script, Lucien had written 'You and me forever.' It was bittersweet, but it made her smile.

Isabella remembered the day in the woods and the man that Lucien had devoured. It had been very exciting for them both, she knew. She recalled the way his eyes looked every time he had looked at her that day: they were filled with trust.

She was the only one Lucien had ever been able to really trust, and now she did not trust him.

She crumpled the paper and tossed it into the waste can next to her desk. Next, she began to transfer all the contents from one purse to the other. It was best to put the past all the way behind her. It was enough just to worry about the present, and the future was endless.

Isabella was just clasping and zipping the bag shut when her mother called her. "Isabella, Lucien is here!"

She took a deep breath and paused. Finally, she stood and slung the bag over her shoulder. She checked her hair and makeup and wound up reapplying lipstick and running a comb through her hair.

"Well, Isabella," she said to her reflection. "You're on."

She arrived downstairs to find only Rose. "Where is Lucien, in with Daddy?"

"Yes, as you should know," Rose said with a smile. "We understand that Rasia is Queen, and Lucien is soon to become Master, but your father is the king of this house and of us. He will have his say with Lucien, but no worries. He is always the diplomatic one, you know."

Isabella nodded and took a seat on a stool at the island in the middle of the kitchen.

"How are you doing, dear?" Rose asked.

She sighed. "I'm fine. A bit nervous, yes, but fine overall."

"Would you like juice or a soda while you wait?"

She shook her head. "I will take a glass of cold water, though."

Her mother brought it to her, and she drank it down quickly. "Now, I guess I should use the bathroom!" The two laughed, and Rose knew Isabella would be okay.

Isabella had just stepped out when Patrick and Lucien came into the kitchen. "Hello, Mrs. Gilliam," Lucien said. "Isabella is not down yet?"

"She is just using the facilities, Lucien," Rose told him with a smile. The boy was certainly growing into a striking man, and he looked just like his father. "She will be out in just a bit."

As if on cue, Isabella entered the room. Lucien's eyes lit up; she just got more and more beautiful with each passing day! He couldn't wait to be alone with her, to talk to her and hear about her life in more detail. It was as if his entire life was all about her, and he wanted to soak up as much of Isabella as he could.

"You are stunning, as always," he said shyly.

She took her bag from the island. "Thank you."

The room went into an awkward silence. Finally, Patrick said, "Well, I suppose you two are getting hungry."

That jerked Lucien to reality. "Yes!" he said, pulling his eyes off Isabella. "Are you ready?"

"I was born ready," she teased. To Patrick and Rose, she said, "See you, two kids, later. Stay out of trouble, and no sweets."

They all had a laugh, and Isabella and Lucien left.

"Wow," she said as they approached his new Jaguar. "Your mom really goes all out."

He nodded as he unlocked the car with the remote, a single alarm emanating from the vehicle. He opened her door for her and held it wide for her to get in. "Yes, you know her: always the show-off."

Isabella made herself comfortable as Lucien got in and started the engine. "It's quite gorgeous, Lucien. I'll bet it's fun to drive."

He put the car in gear and squealed the tires as they left the driveway. "Play your cards right, and you might find out!" He smiled at her, and she smiled back.

Lucien took the long way to the restaurant. He had chosen The Chili Bowl, and as soon as they pulled up, Isabella knew what he had in mind for their lunch. "Chili dogs, Lucien?"

"Yes, Chili dogs, Isabella."

They ate like old friends, laughing and talking, catching up on everything but Lucien's escapades of the last three years. She told him in depth about her interest in the history of the world, and he listened intently. He told her about getting to know Martin better, and Isabella could actually hear a slight affection in his voice for the man.

"How are things between you and your mother?" she finally asked him. "You seem to be getting on quite well."

Lucien finished his last bite and washed it down quickly with a drink of soda. "It is a façade," he told her simply.

"What do you mean?"

"Well," he began, "I get along with her as a means of getting by. I hate her, and she doesn't like me, but it doesn't matter. She is who she is, I am who I am, and contrary to popular opinion, she will not live forever."

Now he had her complete attention. "We will all live forever, Lucien. We are vampires."

"Not Rasia," he told her. "She won't."

"What do you mean?" Isabella knew exactly what he meant. The only way one vampire could die was at the hands of another with more power. What was he planning?

"It's nothing but big dreams, Isabella, that's all," he said.

Now she got the feeling he did not trust her as he once did. Before he would have gotten anything off his chest to her, and she could tell there was something there now. He was not divulging it, however, and that bothered her. She had done nothing to make him doubt her loyalty.

"Tell me, Lucien," she said.

Lucien looked around the restaurant, then gazed back at Isabella. "I have my plans for the future, Isabella, and they do not include Rasia."

"Do you know what you are saying?" she asked him.

"Not only do I know what I am saying, I know my plans." He looked her deep in the eyes. "You are still my Isabella, are you not? I can still trust you as my best friend and confidante?"

"Lucien, you know you can." She was disgusted at the question.

He nodded. "I had to ask, Isabella. It has been a long… time."

They sat quietly as she finished her food, and after the server took away their plates and refilled their soda, Lucien began.

"I am very, very strong now, and I am powerful," he said. "I lived a lie for thirteen years, thinking I was just a strange, sick boy. I was punished by that woman for who I am."

"Did you know that she would walk around me for years, sniffing me? I used to think I smelled bad," he said, "but after I learned the truth, I knew; she wanted to drink my blood. Her own son!"

Isabella cleared her throat. "Lucien, with her being a witch she likely did not understand things clearly for herself. Do you know what I mean?"

"I don't care," he said forcefully. "Her day will come. I will not have that witch hovering over my shoulder when I step into my reign."

"Well, I guess you have to do what you have to do, but you need to think about this long and hard," Isabella said. "There could be serious unforeseen repercussions. What about the Powers?"

"They want her dead too. They are nearly done with her, I feel it."

With that Lucien stood, and the conversation ended abruptly. The black hatred in his eyes disappeared instantly, and he held out his hand to Isabella. "Are you ready for the Smithsonian, little hummingbird?"

She reached out and took it, letting him pull her to her feet. "Hummingbird, huh? I like that."

Soon they were on their way to see history.

∞

The Smithsonian was an amazing place to Lucien, full of interesting and astounding things. Isabella had been right to be interested in the subject. There was so much one could learn in a place like this, he discovered.

Isabella did the leading. They looked at everything from African art to Native American pieces. She talked to him about them all, filling him in on the cultures and the peoples that made or owned the things they viewed.

Lucien saw that Isabella was intelligent, educated, and sensible. She would make a perfect Queen for him. He could hardly wait to taste her skin and make her fully his once again. Only a year to go.

They spent hours walking around looking and finally left the Institute. They decided to have ice cream together in a nearby park before he would return Isabella home. They sat with chocolate sugar cones wrapped in napkins, and they chatted on a park bench.

"When will I see you again?" Lucien asked her, reaching out to wipe ice cream off her nose.

Isabella laughed. "Well, I study all week during the day. Maybe we could go out one evening. What do you think?"

"I think it sounds perfect," he said. "How about if I make plans and surprise you with them?"

"Really?" she was impressed. "When do you want to do this?"

Lucien shrugged. "I don't know. How about Tuesday or Wednesday?"

"Here," she said, handing him her cone. "Hold this." She dug in her bag and pulled out an appointment book. "Wednesday would be good. I have to tutor a girl from Historical Literature on Tuesday night for three hours. Ugh!"

"Does she come to your place?" he asked.

Isabella nodded. "Yes. I tutor her and a couple of other girls in different subjects. It's funny, being only sixteen and having to help the nineteen and twenty-year-olds. I kind of get a kick out of it to tell you the truth."

"Yes," Lucien replied. "I bet you do." He found he was swollen with pride for the girl seated next to him. He looked over at her and saw she had ice cream on her nose again.

"Here you are, tutoring college students, and you can't keep your food off your face."

Isabella wiped her nose once again. "Shut up, Lucien," she said, punching him in the arm.

Yes, it was all going to be good.

∞

They were silent for the entire drive home, but the air was charged up with unsaid words, especially on Isabella's part. Lucien pulled into her driveway and turned to her, his eyes full of love. "I am looking forward to Wednesday already, girl."

"Me too," she replied blushing. Then she straightened up in her seat. "There is something I need to tell you, Lucien."

"Shoot," he said.

She wove her fingers together in her lap. "I still see the real you in there, in your eyes," she began. "And that's okay, don't get me wrong. After all, it is the real you that I love so much."

She continued. "You are coming into a massive role of leadership; it will be a huge responsibility. I believe if you indulge your violent nature all the time, you will be the destruction of life as we all know it."

"Isabella, don't be…"

"No, Lucien," she said sternly. "I need you to listen to me now. Responsibility and doing right by our kind is very important to me, and I expect it to be important to the man I spend eternity with. Do you understand?"

Lucien looked at her. He wasn't sure what she was saying exactly, but he knew it made him squirm. "Are you saying I cannot… have my fun? Even if Rasia is gone?"

"I am saying that having fun is one thing, but doling out utter destruction, all the time, is quite another." She leaned forward and kissed his cheek. "Think about what I am saying and come to your own conclusions, okay?"

Lucien nodded. "Will I see you Wednesday?"

"Only if you show up," she told him, smiling wickedly. She grabbed the door handle and got out of the car, shutting the door behind her.

Lucien watched her walk into the house. Isabella, his ever level-headed Isabella. What he heard her saying was that he had to grow up. Well, that was to be expected.

But once Rasia was gone, he would indeed have his fun. The world would be his playground, and he would take advantage of all the toys it had to offer. Isabella would certainly come around to his way of thinking.

CHAPTER 22

Today was Lucien's seventeenth birthday.

Isabella was very excited. Tonight they would spend his birthday together, just the two of them. No Rasia, no Patrick or Rose, and no Martin. Just Isabella and Lucien. They would have dinner at a restaurant she chose, and they would spend the entire night alone in the guest house on her parents' property.

Yes, tonight was the night she would give herself back to Lucien entirely, and she wanted it to be perfect.

In the past year, Lucien had surprised her with the changes in his behavior. He didn't prowl after other women, and he was always available when she called. In the last few months, they had spent time together nearly every day, and he fawned over her as if she were a precious jewel.

He let her take him to museums and benefits. He soaked up everything she said, and together they would talk for hours and hours. They played, laughed, and sometimes discussed very serious subjects, such as his eighteenth birthday. Things would change drastically then, for Lucien would come into full power. She wanted to know his intentions, and she wanted to familiarize herself with the plans he was making for the world.

The world was a perfect place as it was right now. There was no criminal activity. The Family was tight-knit all over; any place one wanted to visit was open to them. The Family accepted each other with open arms.

This was the one topic Lucien remained tight-lipped about, however. When she would ask his thoughts on future plans, he would tell her only that she would be surprised, for he indeed had grand ideas. He simply didn't want to begin discussing them until he came into full power. He didn't want to jinx himself, so to speak.

Now she was waiting for him to pick her up for their date. She wore a belted white linen dress with matching sandals, and she wore pearls on her neck and in her ears. She gave her hair a quick brush and headed downstairs. She was both excited and nervous.

Lucien was waiting for her when she walked into the living room. Expectant smiles graced the faces of her parents. "I'm ready," she said breathlessly, noticing the gaze of approval on Lucien's face.

Rose gave her daughter a hug. "Okay, then," she said. "I guess we will see you in the morning, then?"

"Yes," Isabella replied. "Are you ready, Lucien?"

"I was born ready," he teased.

She took his arm, and they went to the car. They drove to the restaurant of her choice, Plume, a five-star bistro which she had made reservations for months ago. She had chosen it because they offered a spectacular lamb, which she loved.

Once seated at their table, they ordered wine, Chardonnay for Isabella, and Merlot for Lucien. They put in their orders, and when the waitress left, Lucien immediately took Isabella by the hands. His eyes were smoky with desire.

"I can't believe the time has finally come," he said in a husky voice.

She smiled. "I know. I thought it would never get here myself."

"I have something for you," Lucien said.

He released her hands and reached inside his dinner jacket, withdrawing a small black velvet box. Isabella sucked in her breath and held it. It was just too soon for an engagement!

"Isabella," he began. "My whole life, through bad and good, you have been the one consistent thing, even waiting while I went through my changes."

"Lucien, I…"

"It is the will of the Powers that we are together, you know this," he told her in a matter-of-fact tone.

Isabella nodded. "Yes," she said simply.

Lucien nodded. "It doesn't have to happen tomorrow, but it will happen. We both know it. Nothing would please both of our parents more than to be told we have become engaged. Besides, I have already asked your father, and he approves."

With that, Lucien opened the black box and held it in her direction. The ring inside was breathtaking. It was yellow gold with a large emerald-cut diamond in the center. The main diamond was flanked by two smaller ones of the same cut on either side, and baguettes ran around the entirety of the band.

"So, Isabella, would you marry me someday?" Lucien asked.

She took the box in her hand and gazed at the beautiful ring nestled inside. She looked up at Lucien and said, "You know I will."

With that, he took the box from her and removed the ring. He took her hand softly and placed it on her finger. Then he stood and leaned over, kissing her with great passion.

"You have made me very, very happy, Isabella," he said. "I would do anything for you."

Their food arrived, and it was perfect. They ate holding hands and laughing, and it was as though sex was the furthest thing from their minds, but it was not. Both of them could hardly wait for dessert to be over so they could leave.

Soon enough, they were back on the Gilliams' property. Rose had built a fire in the fireplace at the guest house, and it was warm when they entered.

"Wow," Lucien said. "Your mother really wanted things to be perfect."

There were vases full of red roses all over the place. The bed was made up with a thick silk comforter, and wine was chilling in a bucket next to the bed. They would want for nothing.

"I'm going to go freshen up," Isabella said softly.

Lucien nodded. "You do that."

She left the room and Lucien set about making

things just right. He poured wine and turned the bed down. He then removed all of his clothes except his silk boxers, and then he sat back on the bed against overstuffed pillows. He was anxious and beside himself.

Isabella appeared suddenly in the firelight. She was completely naked, her hair loose with large curls. She stood at the foot of the bed before him and said nothing. Lucien sat up, nearly spilling his wine.

"I poured you some," he said, his voice gruff.

She slowly walked to him. "Thank you," she replied, taking the glass from his hand. She sat next to him on the bed and held his eyes while she drank the wine.

Her scent was overwhelming, sweet and soft. He reached out and cupped her breast, then stroked her nipple with his thumb. She broke out in goosebumps, and a small moan escaped her lips.

"This will be my first time since… since…"

"I know," he said gently.

He took her glass from her and laid her down on the silken sheets. His lips were on hers, and they were suddenly exploring each other's mouths and bodies with unbridled passion. It was all Lucien could do, with a raging erection, to stop things.

He began to kiss her neck, working his way down to her breasts. He took his time there; she smelled so luscious and rich that he was nearly drunk with her. Before Isabella knew what was happening, Lucien's face was between her legs, and he was doing things to her with his tongue that Isabella never even knew existed.

She writhed and moaned with pleasure, her fingers

tangled in his hair. "Oh, Lucien! Oh, my!" She made no effort to stop him, and she couldn't have if she tried. He was fully intoxicated with the fullness of his Isabella.

He loved her with his mouth for a full hour. At one point, he was on his back, and she straddled his face, gently grinding herself against him. Oh, this was far better than he had ever imagined it could be. If there had ever been heaven, this was it.

Then she moved off of him and looked into his eyes. She moved her hips down and brushed herself against his erection while she ran her breasts over his chest. In a flash, she drove herself down on him, and when he was fully inside of her, he cried out.

He would not last long.

She rode him hard, grinding and thrusting, biting and clawing at his skin. He tried to hold back, but this was the one being on the planet he had no control over. He grabbed the sheets in fistfuls and arched his back violently as she slammed her body down on him and held it there. She could feel him throbbing inside of her as he filled her up.

Isabella collapsed on Lucien, and they lay silently together, tasting each other's sweat. It was done. The union was technically complete, and Lucien knew that his heart was hers for all eternity.

He took her by the hair and kissed her on the mouth. Then he looked into her eyes and said playfully, "Are you ready for round two?"

∞

"Lucien, today is an important day," Rasia was

saying to him. "We will be flying to Honduras where you will be shown your father's permanent sanctuary. It is necessary that you know where this is for the safety of you and the Family."

Lucien drained his coffee cup. "What safety? We don't worry about safety here."

Rasia had an annoyed look on her face. How he hated the witch! "You are going to be marrying a girl that has human blood in her veins. We have no idea what this could mean for the world or our people."

"What time are we leaving?" he asked.

Rasia stood from her place at the table. "In one hour. Our flight will leave as soon as we are settled in the plane. Bring a bag, because we will be staying in La Ceiba."

He followed her when she left the room and went up to pack some clothes. He called Isabella. "Hello, my love. I had an outstanding time last night."

"Me too," she told him in a sleepy voice.

The two had been engaged now for ten months, and they spent every free moment together making love and planning for the future.

He continued. "I have to go to Honduras with Mother. I will not be back until tomorrow. Forgive me?"

"Of course," she said. "Be good while you are there, love."

"I will. I love you," he told her. "I'll see you soon."

With that Lucien hung up and prepared a bag for the trip. His father's sanctuary? It sounded like ridiculousness to him.

Soon they were on their way to the airport, where their private plane was ready and waiting. In no time, they were on board listening to their pilot welcome them and gush all over them, which made him sick. He just wanted to get this over with and get back home to Isabella.

He sat back and closed his eyes as the plane took off. His thoughts went to her taste and her scent, and he found himself in heaven all over again. He could hardly wait to have her again.

∞

"Alright, Lucien," Rasia was saying. "We will simply jump, and the rest will come naturally to you. It is time."

They were standing on the very edge of a cliff, with waters rushing violently below them. He knew there would come a time when his mother would be informing him of the more thrilling aspects of his heritage, and she had always told him he would be able to fly when his powers increased. He was excited; today was the day.

She continued. "When we hit the water, keep me in your sights. All you need to do is follow me, and I will take you to where we are going." She paused for a minute, looking at him. "Are you ready?"

"Yes," he said, and with that, they both leaped off the cliff into the raging sea below.

Lucien fell toward the water fast, his mother right beside him. He was aware that he was controlling his fall without even trying. He looked at Rasia. She was smiling, her red hair flying behind her.

They cut through the water like a pair of knives, and then Rasia was swimming at a high rate of speed. He kept up with her easily, and though he knew he could pass her easily, he let her continue to lead. A large hole in the rock appeared before them, and they swam into it.

In minutes they were swimming through another, smaller hole, then suddenly the water ended. Lucien shot out of it and landed on the rock on his feet. Rasia stood smiling.

"Fun, yes?" she asked him.

He nodded and shook his hair out. "Superb."

Now they ran, and they ran fast. There was a corridor-like passage which they passed through, and now Lucien did pass his mother. He passed her with such power and speed that she was alarmed. It frightened her somewhat, though she was not sure why.

Lucien suddenly came to the heart of the cave, and as soon as he entered its hollowness, the place lit up with candles, just like his father's office had. He turned, but his mother was not there; he had left her behind.

She arrived quickly, though, and as he gazed around in wonder, she began to speak.

"This is it," she said. "This is where your father came for centuries when they wanted to kill him. It is also where he began the family we have now. He came here for solitude in later days, as you may desire. It is yours now."

She sat in a large high back chair in the middle of

the large room and closed her eyes, resting. Lucien looked at her for only a moment, and he knew immediately that the time had come.

He rushed at her full force, his feet lifting off the ground as he took flight. His body slammed into hers, knocking the chair over backward. He righted himself and landed on his feet facing her, waiting for her to rise to her feet.

Rasia stood and shook herself off. "You rotten bastard," she sneered, her eyes on fire. "I am going to kill you dead."

Now she rushed at him, but he simply swung on her and stopped her in her tracks. The impact of his arm knocked her thirty feet, and she crashed into the hard stone wall of the cave. A single candle fell to the floor, but it remained lit.

"I find myself wondering," Lucien said as he began to pace before her, "who is going to kill who."

Now a look of intense fear crossed Rasia's face. He was strong, stronger than she ever would have imagined. She needed time to think, but she knew he would not afford her that.

"Rasia, I want to thank you," Lucien continued. "Thank you for lying to me all my life. Thank you for imprisoning me in my own home and making me feel like a freak. Thank you, thank you."

The two rushed toward each other now, and both took flight. They slammed together in mid-air, clawing and striking each other with fierce fury. It spun them around in circles as they fought.

But Rasia was tiring fast, and Lucien was just getting started. He picked her up from the ground and threw her here and there like a rag doll. She was bloodied and bruised, and she had ceased fighting back.

She knew this was her end.

Now she lay crumpled on the floor of the cave, her breathing heavy and ragged. Lucien straddled her and sat upon her beaten body. He took her by the hair and turned her face toward his. "Look at me, bitch!"

Rasia opened her eyes and smiled at her son. Even now she could smell him. She should have feasted on this animal long ago.

"This is for my father," he said, and then ripped her head straight off, just as she had done to the Master, Cyril.

Her body fell limp to the floor, and Lucien looked at the head in his hands. The eyes were wide with surprise, and the smile was gone, nothing but a wide, silent scream remaining.

He threw her head across the cave, then he dined on her blood for a while. Finally, he took off flying through the corridor of the cave, back toward the sea.

He was going to have a bit of fun while he was visiting Honduras.

∞

"Lucien, what have you done?" Isabella was behind him. When she had arrived, he did not know.

He turned the chair he sat in to face her. "What do you mean?"

Isabella began to pace. "First you tell me your

mother has died in an accident in Honduras like I am too damn stupid to know what you did. Then it is all over the television that the entire area there has gone up in flames. They cannot even count the bodies of our dead Family!"

Lucien closed his eyes against her verbal onslaught. "I don't know. Maybe someone was smoking in bed."

"Don't lie to me!" she screamed. "You are eighteen in one month, and you have done nothing but wreak havoc the world over! What the heck are you doing?"

Now he stood and walked to her, taking her face in his hands. "I am just having a little fun, Isabella. I think it is out of my system now."

"I hope so," she told him. "Right now, we have Family fighting and rioting, murdering each other all over, and you have done nothing to amend it. You went to California under the guise of bringing peace, and as soon as you left, the body count skyrocketed. The people are reveling in the violence!"

Lucien turned and stood before the fire in the family room. "I am due to go to Spain on a flight tomorrow to deal with the violence there. I will make it right."

"Well," she began, her voice calmer. "I am scheduled to go with my father to Germany for one month to deal with the chaos there, as you remember. You scheduled my trip."

"Yes, Isabella, and I appreciate all your help."

Now she walked around to face him. "This is how it will be, Lucien DeSai. Are you listening closely?"

He stared into her eyes and nodded. "I will return

the evening before you come into full power, we will spend that evening together, and celebrate your eighteenth birthday," she said.

"Yes?" he replied.

"You will decide by then if you want me, or if you want this… this destruction. You will not have both," she said calmly.

Lucien smiled. "If we died together, would it not be perfect?"

Isabella slapped him hard across the face. His hand went to his face, surprised.

"This, or me. Destruction or life eternally with me," she began. "I will die if you see fit but know that we will not be together if that is the final outcome. You will go down with this world alone."

Isabella walked away from him. She stopped at the door. "I will sleep at my parents' tonight; we are leaving for Germany before dawn. If you choose life, the people will follow. If you choose death, well, why send me then?"

With that, she was gone, and Lucien sat back down in the chair.

She was right, the world was in utter chaos, but he loved it. The bloodshed and the anger were like a wonderful meal to him, and he wanted it to continue. He planned to set the world aflame in its entirety, on his eighteenth birthday. It would only take one breath from his mouth to do so. The Powers had given him such strength.

But he had never envisioned dying alone. He had

some romantic picture of the planet going down while he held the hand of his beloved Isabella, but he knew she would not comply. She was furious.

He had a choice to make.

But, he had a month to make it. In the meantime, while she was away, he would enjoy the carnage. He would even incite more of it in Spain, and maybe he would stay a few days to watch the party. The thought made him laugh out loud.

He had plenty of time to watch things go up in smoke…

CHAPTER 23

The room was dark, the only light being eighteen candles that burned brightly on top of a chocolate cake covered in raspberry glaze.

Isabella stood, beautiful in red, across the table from him. She had just arrived that evening from Germany, where things had seemed to calm down a bit. She looked stunning. She would celebrate his biggest birthday with him, and she would expect to hear his decision.

Lucien approached her from the other side of the table. "You are striking, my Isabella."

"Have you come to a conclusion?" She asked seriously. She would not be deterred by flattery.

Lucien nodded. "I have. I will save it for after the cake."

They stood silent, both of them watching the candles burn in the darkness. Finally, Isabella spoke. "I bought you a gift in Germany," she told him without looking at him.

She turned around and dug through her bag. When she turned back to him, she held a small white box with a red ribbon on it.

"Happy eighteenth birthday, Lucien. You have always been the love of my life."

He took the box. "Thank you, Isabella." With that, he pulled on the ribbon and removed it. He then took the cover off the box and gazed at the gift inside.

It was a large gold ring. Two gold dragons made up the band, and they were obviously making love. Their eyes were rubies, and there was a tiny black onyx on each dragon in the place its heart would be.

Lucien removed the ring and put it on the pinky finger of his right hand; it fit perfectly. It was exquisite, and he looked up at her with his eyes filled with love.

"Thank you, Isabella," he said.

After a moment, he spoke again. "As soon as the candles are blown out, I come into power. It is finally time."

A chill ran over the back of his future bride. "Yes, Lucien, and I am hoping for the very best, for all eternity."

"I am ready," he told her, "are you? Midnight is almost here, the very time of my birth. I am counting down."

"I was born ready."

Lucien reached across the table and took both of her hands in his. He looked into her eyes for a long moment, and she gazed into his. Suddenly he looked down at the cake and the flickering candles.

"I love you, Isabella, with all my soul. Count with me."

So together they counted down to the midnight

hour. "Five, four, three, two…"

As the clock chimed twelve o'clock, Lucien DeSai let out a slight puff of his breath, and the candles flickered into darkness.

ENTREATY

This book was made possible by reviews from readers like you. Reviews fuel my creativity. If you enjoyed this novel, I implore you to please write a review and share your experience on the retailer's website. The livelihood for authors is entirely dependent on reviews, and I must say, it is the largest obstacle as a struggling author that I have encountered. Please tell a friend, tell a loved one about this read. With your help, I will be one step closer to overcoming this obstacle. In return, I thank you from the bottom of my heart, and sincerely appreciate your time and effort.

Humbled, with gratitude,

R.W.K. Clark

ABOUT THE AUTHOR

I am a father of two beautiful children, Jon and Kim. They are my motivating forces; they are the lighthouse in this vast ocean. In my life, they are the air that I breathe; they are the oasis in this desert of uncertainty. They are my greatest joy in life and my number one priority. I have a long list of hobbies, and I attribute that to my lust for life! I like to surround myself with positive people, who share the same interests. Family values, the arts, outdoors, nature, and travel are tops on my list. I embrace attending cultural and artistic events because I believe dramatic self-expression is the window to the soul. I wear my heart on my sleeve, and I still believe in chivalry, and I always treat people the way I want to be treated.

www.rwkclark.com

www.ingramcontent.com/pod-product-compliance
Lightning Source LLC
Chambersburg PA
CBHW022133190626
46810CB00016B/609